Elements & Flame

The Elemental Series Book 1: An Amber Mountain Novel

Jillian Beane

Jillian Beane LLC

Library of Congress Control Number: 2024902706

ISBN: 979-8-9900217-1-6 (Paperback)

ISBN: 979-8-9900217-0-9 (eBook)

Book Cover by Shawnna Sue

Paperback Wrap by Alt19 Creative

Editing by Dayna Hart at Hart to Heart Edits

Proofread by Angela Garcia of Romance the Page LLC

1st edition 2024

Published by Jillian Beane LLC

Jillian Beane LLC

PO Box 10

Mechanicsburg, Ohio 43044

Contents

Prologue

Carefully, mindful of her injuries, Suleima slowly picked her way through the rough terrain, leaning heavily on a long stick for support and balance. Her supplies drifted along behind her, inches above the ground. Although the sky was just beginning to darken, the canopy of the trees obscured any light from reaching the forest floor. She reached out her senses, feeling a few small creatures waking for the night, while others were bedding down around her. There was no immediate danger.

She took a deep breath. Her friend had scouted out the area before she arrived. There was a werewolf pack somewhere in the area, but no other supernaturals frequented this region—a smaller town, surrounded by a lot of forested area. It would be a great spot for her to rest and heal.

The wounds on the left side of her body, face, and arm pulled painfully with every step, but her mind was solely focused on getting to her destination, so she could protect herself and concentrate on healing. Anything beyond a shallow breath still threatened to double her over. Broken ribs were not an injury she ever wished to repeat.

If she thought she could get back up, she would have bent to kiss the ground when the cabin came into view. Home. The abandoned cabin was barely visible, the growth of the forest hiding its features a natural camouflage.

She dropped the magic she was using to haul her supplies along behind her and approached a tree about twenty-five yards from the cabin. Placing her hand on the trunk, she closed her eyes and imagined a circle around the perimeter of the cabin to this tree and pushed her will and intention. She was out of breath when she closed the spell, completing the protection ward that she had placed. It would have to be enough for now. Her body wouldn't allow her to bend and bury her fingers in the dirt to perform the spell more efficiently.

She continued to the doorway of the cabin, pulling her supplies behind her again. It took more effort than she wanted to admit getting up the few steps that led to the covered porch. But she smiled when she got the door open. Her friend had added some supplies and set up some comfortable rustic furniture for her to use. She closed the door with a push of air and laid her head against it. Closing her eyes, she placed another minor ward around the door and walls of the cabin, a final measure of protection, and then lay on the bed. Tomorrow, she would venture out around the property for the healing herbs she felt growing around the grounds of her new cabin and the surrounding area. But tonight, she drifted off into a much-needed healing sleep.

Chapter 1

Just like every morning for the last six months, Suleima woke early and checked the wards surrounding her home. As usual, nothing had been disturbed. She reached out her senses, finding all the creatures of the forest moving about as they usually did. The nocturnal animals were bedding down, while the others were emerging from their homes in search of their food for the day.

She pushed her will at the coals in the stove, fanning the flames with air to heat some water for her breakfast. She winced at the stiffness of the joints in her left arm and hand as she stretched and then dressed for the day and braided her long dark hair. Each day she felt a little better, a little stronger, physically. But there would always be lingering consequences from her injuries, which seemed only fitting. The psychological scars, though invisible, were so much worse.

She went about tidying her home and taking inventory of her herbs and supplies, so she could forage for the things she needed on her walk later in the day.

The hike would help with her tracking skills, allow her to replenish her supplies, and give her some much-needed exercise. Her stamina was almost back to normal, but each day, she was sure to venture farther and longer than the day before.

Tracking a doe through the forest, Suleima could feel the earth breathing beneath her feet. There was nowhere near the connection to the earth and her elements in the city that she'd found here in her new home. Here, she was on her own, and away from the rapid pace of the city, away from her past, and she preferred it that way.

There was a squirrel foraging for nuts to the west, a snake sunning on a rock somewhere to the south. A pack of predators were a couple miles north—too far to judge the species. Using the earth's essence more than her own sight, she could see the trees. Each individual leaf pulsed and vibrated with the slight breeze in the air, straining for the sun. The screech of a hawk, soaring above, brought her back to her task.

Using the vibrations, the ebb and flow of the earth and her elements, she was able to silently track the doe deep into the forest to a small clearing just beside a shallow creek. Even that small trickle of water was enough to make her muscles sing. If not for the rain last night, the creek would likely be dry. She crouched, placing her right hand on the ground, physically connecting with the soil below. Her fingers tingled and her blood raced. As the power of the elements raced through her, she knew her eyes had drifted from their usual gray to a vibrant violet.

Suleima basked in the warmth of the sun, filtered through the leaves of the trees behind her. Taking a deep breath, Suleima released the energy she was holding while touching the soil, and slowly stood. She retraced her steps out of the clearing and headed in the direction of her home. She had waited too long to use the elements; she was tired and needed to recharge.

She never should have let it go for this long. She needed to keep her skills honed. Although she was away from the city, the reason she left was still out there, and her past would catch up with her sooner or later. Hearing a slight huff to her left, she cursed herself for letting her guard down. The pack of predators she sensed earlier had closed in on her without her knowing it. Wolves . . . *werewolves.*

She had known there was a pack nearby, but this would be her first encounter with them. As they came into view, she noticed the unusual markings on the lead wolf. The Alpha. He was gray, but one eye was ringed with black, the black fur trailing down through his cheek, down to his neck, reminding her of a scar. One hip was black, and he had black rings down part of his tail. His piercing eyes were gray-blue. He was larger than the few wolves she had come into contact with before. If he had been standing next to her, his back would have lined up with her hip.

The pack fanned out behind him, those that were visible, anyway. Suleima opened her senses and felt the others at her back and flanks. There wasn't aggression, just wariness and alertness. She could feel one lonely wolf behind the rest, out of sight.

When the woman with jet-black hair came into view, she was wearing a barely-there top and mini shorts, in contrast to Suleima's dark jeans and long-sleeved green shirt beneath her leather jacket. Suleima lowered her eyes, not wanting to meet the eyes of the predator in perceived challenge. "Hello." She spoke softly. With their enhanced hearing, everyone in the pack, including those out of sight, would hear.

"We won't hurt you, unless threatened." The woman's voice had a gravelly note to it, and Suleima wondered if it was due to her recent change or to chronic smoking.

"Likewise," Suleima said, careful to keep her gaze downcast. She could feel at least twenty wolves spread out around her but sensed a connection with more. At the very edge of the wolves, there was something else. Something she had hoped to never see again.

"Stay back!" she shouted, running in the direction of the new threat, though running from the pack was dangerous in and of itself. Predators chased prey, and that is how she would present to the wolves right now, but two of the pack members were in serious danger. Suleima raced past the wolves, using her ability to sense where they were to dodge their attempts to stop her, pulling at her power over earth to increase her speed. She wouldn't be able to keep the pace up for long, but the threat was closing in, and there was no time to pause and explain.

As the last of the wolves came into view, and sensing the rest of the pack closing in behind her, Suleima dropped to the ground, sliding between two wolves, narrowly missed by their snapping jaws. Reaching one hand up, she grabbed air, the other hand slammed into the ground, and she shouted, "Reveal!"

The glamour dropped from the orc, whose throat was in her raised hand, alerting the wolves to the threat.

Suleima pulled with her powers, and vines from nearby plants snaked in her direction, wrapping around the arms of the orc, pulling taut, immobilizing its frantic and violent thrashing. Most of the damage from the orc's claws were mitigated by Suleima's thick leather coat. The whole of the wolf pack was around her now; the Alpha snarling viciously, and the woman in human form stood at his shoulder. A final vine descended from the tree above, wrapped around the orc's neck and jerked violently up, breaking it.

Taking a deep breath, she slid from her position under the orc and slowly stood. "I apologize for this, Alpha. Once I sensed the orc, there was no time to warn you. It was headed straight for these wolves." She nodded to indicate the pair standing together to her left.

A black wolf approached from her left, snapping its jaws at her, a couple of other wolves at its flanks. All three wolves growled, baring their large fangs.

The Alpha pinned his ears back and put himself between Suleima and his wolves, a vicious rumble cowing the three aggressive wolves as well as the rest of the pack.

Suleima released the breath that she had been holding since the black wolf approached and nodded her thanks as the three aggressive wolves trotted quickly away from the pack.

"Excuse me one more moment, please." She turned her back to the Alpha and knelt, sinking her fingers into the dirt. "You have come, and now you'll go. A trace of none where wild things grow." Smoke rose from the dirt, surrounding the body. The forest, which had been silent since the appearance of the orc, began to come alive. Rustling leaves and the twitter of birds, sounds familiar and comforting. Rain fell, dissipating the smoke, revealing the start of a young sapling where none had been before.

When Suleima turned back, the look of shock on the woman's face was easy to read, but she quickly replaced it with an impassive mask. She spoke again, as if the incident with the orc was nothing out of the ordinary. "We are The Amber Mountain Pack. We heard rumors of your presence and wanted to introduce ourselves." Hesitantly, the woman continued. "We have heard of your past troubles . . ."

"And you wanted to warn me to keep it out of your territory." Knowing it was a stupid move, Suleima turned her back on the predators, dismissing them. "Got it."

The Alpha growled menacingly.

Suleima stopped and turned back to face the pack. Her fingers itched to connect to the earth, and the hair on the back of her neck stood on end.

The woman seemed to cower at the anger radiating from the Alpha, even as Suleima sensed he reined in that anger because of its effect on the pack. "We know what you were up against and what you were trying to do. It has come to us from Pack Setura. We do not wish to have a similar incident here, but we will offer any assistance to you that we can."

"Thank you," Suleima said gratefully, "This is the first I have seen an unnatural since I arrived here. It does seem that things may be starting all over again." She hoped the dejection she felt wasn't visible on her face.

"Thank *you* for this." She indicated the area where the sapling now stood with a wave of her hand. "We will not keep you any longer, but we are sure our paths will cross again." The dark-haired woman walked backwards several steps before turning to walk away at an angle, so her back was never directly toward Suleima, despite the fact her Alpha and pack were still on guard.

Suleima nodded at the Alpha before exiting in the same fashion.

The tension didn't leave Suleima until she was nearly home. Once her home was visible, she crouched and buried her fingers to the first knuckle. She closed her eyes and hummed a low note. The protections she'd placed around her home were undisturbed. She pushed a bit of her remaining power into the ground to strengthen those same protections.

It took effort to pull her fingers from the ground, severing her direct connection with the earth. She was extremely lucky. Her power was dangerously low, and she wouldn't have been able to fight off more than a couple wolves had they decided to attack. She desperately needed to recharge. And she needed to make sure she never allowed herself to get so drained in the future.

Brushing the dirt from her fingers, she curled them against her body to stem the tingling and walked straight into her tiny cabin. The old log cabin with leaded windows was barely visible to anyone who did not already know it was there. Moss covered the roof, and vines had long ago covered the exterior walls. The bed of old leaves covered the ground straight up to the small front porch with weathered wood that blended right in. It was nestled between two huge trees, whose canopy helped keep the cabin cool in the hottest of days.

She called a bird to her using her power over air and sent it with a message to her dearest friend. "An orc. A few miles from home. Gather any information about their movements that you can and return this bird, please."

Inside, Suleima walked to the large, ornate cabinet in the corner beside the old pump sink and opened the saloon style doors wide. She pulled out three vials and set them on the countertop.

She opened the first vial: soil harvested from the grounds of her new home. She poured a small amount into her hand, allowing it to run between her fingers and into an unpainted ceramic bowl below. The cool dirt soothed her frazzled nerves. The encounter with the wolves had unsettled her more than she realized. She rubbed her hands together to mark both palms with the remaining soil.

The water pump was stiff when she began pumping, but soon she had a steady flow of water directly from the ground. She placed her hands palms down under the stream, to avoid washing off the soil, and allowed a small amount into a second ceramic bowl.

Her primary and secondary strengths started, Suleima opened the second vial. The smell of cloves surrounded her. Air, the counter to her primary earth. Four drops of incense into the bowl with the soil, a quiet push of will, and smoke rose, the soil bubbling as if a liquid.

She removed a small piece of charcoal from the third vial and placed it in the bowl with the water and used her pestle to grind the charcoal fine. Another slight push of will, and it also started to smoke. The smoke from both bowls mingled together, forming a fog that quickly filled the room.

Inhaling deeply, Suleima took the fog into her lungs and closed her eyes, visualizing her body slowly filling with the elements. With each breath, her reservoir of power refilled. The fog snaked up in tendrils to lick at her fingers, gathering in an orb in each palm. She released the orbs and they floated into the air above her as the next pair formed.

Four orbs, floating north, south, east, and west to hover in the corner of the cabin corresponding to their direction.

In the center of the room, she took a deep breath and opened her eyes. One loud clap above her head, and the fog vanished immediately, but the four orbs slowly dissipated, the tendrils floating up and toward the center of the room where they gathered at the peak of the ceiling into a cloud that rained colored sparks. She stretched out her arms, catching the sparks, feeling the prickle as each was absorbed. She whispered a quiet thanks for the elements and the power they provided, and released the concentration and power required for the ritual.

Cloud gone, she collapsed onto her bed and into a deep, blessed sleep.

Chapter 2

It was nearly dawn when she awoke, groggy and achy. Too long had she gone without recharging; she couldn't risk doing it ever again. He would find her sooner or later.

Something told her it was likely sooner.

She stretched as she stood, working out the final aches and pains.

A sudden prickle of awareness alerted her to the presence of something nearing her protections. She reached out her senses—a bird flew high above her cabin, a squirrel scrambled away from the path and up a tree. A predator was the cause of its alarm. A large predator.

Werewolf.

Suleima stepped onto her porch and could feel the wolf changing. She stayed where she was, waiting for him to emerge. A second werewolf, in wolf form, stood guard next to the changing man.

About ten minutes later, the man emerged from the brush and toward her cabin. Suleima stepped off the porch to meet him. The Alpha from the pack yesterday. He possessed the same blue-gray eyes as he did in his wolf form. He wore denim shorts and a fitted black t-shirt, despite the chilly temperature of the new dawn.

"Alpha," she said in greeting, keeping her eyes averted so as not to challenge him.

"Name is Gage Hamill." He stopped a few feet in front of her. "I decided to come by and speak to you myself. Running into you yesterday was a surprise to us all."

"I appreciate your offer of help. I had hoped the trouble I experienced in Upper State wouldn't follow me here, but I also understood it was unlikely."

"Very unlikely," he confirmed. "News from Pack Setura indicates a gathering of unnaturals headed in our direction. I assume you didn't leave a forwarding address, but he is tracking you. It will likely be a few more weeks before they make it this far, but make no mistake, they are on their way."

"I'm sorry to bring this to your doorstep. That orc was likely just a scout. There will be more of them, especially once he doesn't return. I sincerely apologize for startling you and the pack yesterday. If there had been any time, I would have given more warning."

Gage nodded. "We have heard a few details from the incident in Upper State. My pack understands this battle is necessary, and we hope that any assistance we can provide will be helpful to finish this conflict. We cannot allow this man to attain his goal. Although there is much bigotry against supernaturals and unnaturals, we cannot allow any of them to attack the naturals. Neither side has the right to dominate the other."

"I agree." Suleima took a deep breath. It was hard to trust, but the Amber Mountain Pack were among the supernaturals on the side of peace. "Would you and your wolf care to come in? I could provide some additional details."

Gage seemed a bit taken aback at the mention of the other wolf, but he covered his surprise well. "All of my pack needs to be aware of the dangers. We would like you to come to our pack house. Tonight."

It wasn't a question.

She bristled at the command. "Provide me with directions and a time, and I will do my best to be there." Her response was likely to aggravate him, and she was enjoying it. She was not part of his pack and wasn't going to take orders from him. It was best he learned that early on.

"Be at this address at seven. No later." He handed her a piece of paper from his shorts pocket. The vein pulsing at his neck was enough of a giveaway; the magical sense of his ire was just a bonus. He turned on his heel and stalked away, stopping near the other wolf to change.

Suleima waited until he was loping down the side of the mountain before she headed back into the cabin, a slight smile on her face. Interactions with the Alpha were going to be fun.

Dressed in jeans, boots, and her leather coat, she felt ready to face the evening. She walked the half mile in the twilight darkness, made darker by the canopy of trees, to her old pickup truck. Primer-gray and dented in several places, it looked abandoned. She pulled it onto the old dirt road and headed toward town.

She was still about ten minutes from town when she turned down a private, paved road. Another two miles of woods and fields led to a large Victorian house with a wide wraparound porch painted white and a three-car garage right next to it. The drive led up to the house and widened to allow for a lot of parking. There were nearly no empty spots. As she stepped out of the truck, she took a deep breath, pulling in awareness of her surroundings. There were no fewer than sixty werewolves around. About half of them were in the house, three were on the front porch watching her arrival, and the remaining wolves were scattered around the property.

As she approached the porch, she recognized the woman who spoke with her during their first encounter. She nodded a greeting before entering the front door, held open by a tall and muscular male. Gage waited inside the door at the entrance to what looked like a very large living room. He glanced pointedly at the clock on the wall and gestured for her to enter the room. She sat in the only chair available, center stage to all the other chairs in the room. All of the pack watched her with caution. The three members from the porch had followed her in to stand at the doorway, just behind their Alpha. Although it was a large room, the number of people inside made her feel claustrophobic.

Gage introduced the woman from their first encounter as Kaly, and Suleima could see the reason for her gravelly voice. A huge scar crossed her throat. A werewolf bite. It was a wonder the woman was alive, let alone able to speak.

"So, now that Suleima has finally arrived, let us get to the reason we have invited her here. A threat is making its way into our territory. A threat Suleima has faced before. We need to familiarize ourselves with this coming threat, so we can come up with the best course of action." He paused, his gaze landing on one group of the pack sitting in the back corner of the room. "Suleima, the floor is yours."

"I'd first like to apologize for bringing this threat to your territory—" She was interrupted by some snide comments. The growl that came next was unmistakably Gage, causing the group to cower, and the hair to stand up on the back of her neck. She tried to ignore the rising tension and continued. "I will do my best to keep everyone in your pack safe.

"I guess I should start at the beginning. I was trained in magic by my mentor, Erist, alongside another student, Dirrin. As people began finding out about supernaturals, Dirrin became more and more against the naturals. Dirrin was cruel to anyone without powers. When our mentor turned his back on him, refusing to continue his training until Dirrin changed, Dirrin lost all sense of who he had been.

"We hadn't heard from him for nearly three years, when he suddenly appeared at Erist's home. Erist cast a spell to hide me and gave me orders not to move or interfere in any way. I watched Dirrin murder our mentor before destroying nearly all of Erist's spell books. Erist was a powerful shaman. I had never met a more powerful man. But Dirrin had changed . . ." Suleima took a deep breath to center herself, the memories brought all of her emotions to the fore, which was dangerous for her as well as the wolves.

She blocked out the tension, hostility, and compassion she felt from the wolves in the room. "I learned later that Dirrin found a new mentor who shared Dirrin's hatred of the naturals. A mentor Dirrin sacrificed in an ancient ceremony he'd found perusing the library his mentor kept. This sacrifice enabled Dirrin to absorb the powers of not only his mentor, but all those his mentor had killed, which was not a small number.

"Dirrin's ultimate goal is to rid the world of naturals and all those he believes do not support his cause. He had gathered a huge number of unnaturals. He had some wolves, though not many, goblins, orcs, banshees, harpies, and many more in his arsenal. I'd done my best to continue my studies using the books I was able to save from Erist's home. I gathered what allies I could, a few other shamanistic students, the mentors I could convince Dirrin was a true threat, and a few other factions who opposed Dirrin's goals. Most were killed or injured in our battle with Dirrin. We faced his minions in small battles several times. Dirrin had intended to work a powerful black magic spell over a small community outside of Setura. If it worked to kill all of the naturals in the community, not only would it rid the world of some naturals, but their deaths would increase his power, allowing him to cast the spell again. Enough deaths, and he could start targeting larger and larger groups.

"In the last battle, Dirrin had used his black magic, sacrificing nearly a third of his minions to basically give the remaining minions super-powers. They were nearly invincible. The battle raged into the night, depleting our forces. I had found and used the spell Erist had cast on me the night he was killed. I was able to slink through the ranks of his minions and managed to flank Dirrin. We fought for what seemed like forever. I was unable to kill him; he had acquired too much power. I did manage to injure him. He went dormant, though I'm not sure where. I was in no condition to pursue him. I left as soon as I was able. There are things in this part of the country I needed to complete my healing. I knew he would not give up on his plan. Being near death would only spur him to gather more power and try again." Suleima took a deep breath and raised her eyes to the Alpha, careful not to meet his gaze directly and nodded.

He responded with a curt nod and then turned to address his pack. "This battle is inevitable and nearly on our doorstep. We need to make a decision." He turned back to Suleima. "Thank you for coming to us this evening to provide details of this threat. We will be in touch."

Essentially dismissed, several pack members gathered in close, crowding her out of the room, and eventually, the house. Once the door closed behind her, Suleima muttered, "I guess that is my cue," and thought she heard Gage snicker in response.

Suleima stepped off the porch and walked about ten feet before realizing she was being followed. She turned to find Kaly behind her. She gave a friendly smile and continued to her car, trying to ignore the prickling sensation being followed caused. As she reached the edge of the main yard of the house, just a few feet from her car, she paused and turned to Kaly.

"I can place a protection around the house. It will not harm any of the wolves who belong to your pack, but it will alert the pack and I if it is crossed. Please ask your Alpha if that is acceptable. I can return at any time to place it, if he is agreeable." Suleima did her best not to grit her teeth at the formality needed to address an unfamiliar pack. She'd rarely had to use the proper form when addressing supernaturals in Setura.

"It is acceptable. Do it now." Her answer was nearly immediate, startling Suleima, and it must have shown on her face, because Kaly continued quietly. "My injury left me unable to communicate verbally for quite a long time." She indicated the scar on her throat. "I developed an extraordinary psychic connection with my Alpha."

Suleima nodded and walked to the edge of the driveway, just past her truck. "My magic can be uncomfortable for wolves. You may wish to return to the house and make sure the wolves watching the perimeter either follow you or are, at the very least, prepared. I do not wish to be attacked tonight."

Kaly nodded but stayed where she was. A moment later, a howl rang out from the woods behind the house. The front door opened, and Gage walked out onto the porch.

"Go ahead," Kaly stated.

"Suit yourself. Just be prepared for some burning and prickling. Shouldn't be unbearable, though it isn't terribly comfortable, I've been told." Suleima knelt, buried her fingers to the first knuckle, and drew in a deep breath. The pulse of the earth sang in her veins. Despite the darkness surrounding her, each blade of grass shone as if the sun was providing a spotlight for it alone. She could sense raccoons and owls hiding in their trees, safe from the predator wolves scattered all around the house and yard. She felt more than heard the gasp from Kaly and assumed her eyes had changed to bright violet. She pushed her will into the ground. In her mind's eye, she drew a circle around the house and yard to the edge of the woods backed up to the property. She sensed the wolves feeling her magic as she pushed it into the ground and it surrounded them. Gage's hands curled into fists; Kaly stiffened her knees, tilted her head back, and deepened her breathing. Several wolves on the other side of the house howled. Suleima did her best to ignore all of the distractions the wolves provided and concentrated on the spell as she cast it.

When it was properly strengthened, Suleima gave a deep sigh, let go of the power, and slowly withdrew her fingers. She stood up and gave Kaly a slight smile. "I'll have to come back at least once a week to strengthen the spell."

Through gritted teeth, Kaly said, "Great. We will make sure there are as few wolves around as possible for the rest of these sessions."

"That is probably best."

Chapter 3

She was bone tired when she climbed out of her car and headed toward the cabin she now called home. She picked a few more herbs along the way. She would need them to continue with her healing rituals she'd been performing since leaving Setura. She'd also need to perform the Ritual of Alucenia again. It had taken a good deal of power to put the ward over the wolves' compound. There'd been a lot of ground to cover.

She had gone too far from the path and was a fair distance from home when she got the familiar prickle of warning; someone or something was trying to pass through her wards. Pulling on her powers, she brought her surroundings into focus as if it was noon, instead of nearing midnight. She could sense the forest animals—some in slumber, others awake and hunting. She could see nothing out of place, but she felt a ripple of wrongness. Suleima took off running toward her cabin, concerned about the power she was using to see in the dark, but she needed to get to her wards before her enemy got through.

Nearing her wards, she smelled the pungent scent of burned sulfur. It was beyond her protection wards but had not yet broken through the wards around her home. She focused on the ripple, trying to bring it into focus.

A banshee. She wasn't nearly powerful enough to break through the wards on Suleima's home, and her intense concentration on her task allowed Suleima to get closer.

Banshees, although not powerful, were extremely difficult to harm or kill. Not much more than a spirit trapped on earth, they were used mainly as messengers of a death soon to come. Dirrin used them to haunt and torture those he planned to come after, a psychological attack. But the last time she had seen one, in Setura, Dirrin had figured out how to make them take corporeal form.

This one was tearing at the wards Suleima had set on her home. Suleima drove her hand into the ground and pushed her will. The dirt just in front of her porch stirred, the leaves separated, and a hand of earth rose from it. Reaching out, it grabbed the banshee by the leg and dragged it off the porch to a small clearing in the middle of the yard, away from the wards it was attempting to damage. Suleima pulled the moisture from the earth and air to form a spear of water. She took aim and thrust the spear into the heart of the banshee. A wail escaped the injured creature.

The banshee shifted from her corporeal form, escaping from the hand of earth, but the iron in the ground had left a burn on her leg. Suleima conjured a small tornado of dirt and aimed it at the banshee. As it surrounded her, the banshee wailed in pain, nearly collapsing Suleima's control. Suleima pulled at her spell, drawing the banshee into the earth, burying her from the waist down in the ground.

Suleima approached cautiously, her focus centered on blocking the banshee's wails, which could cause spontaneous bleeding and death.

Taking more effort than she wished, Suleima pulled the air from the banshee's lungs, silencing her.

Denied her one weapon, the banshee returned to her corporeal form, despite being trapped. She struck out, raking her sharp nails over the sleeve of Suleima's leather coat. Suleima pulled a large, sharp shard of obsidian from the ground. Using its bladelike edge, she slid it through the neck of the banshee, severing the head. Just before it fell away, Suleima pushed her will into the creature and spoke. "Banish wicked creature, harm no one again." Smoke poured from the space in the ground as the body and head of the banshee disappeared.

Suleima dropped to her knees. They'd found her.

She took a deep breath. No physical damage, besides a headache from the banshee's screams before she was able to block them. Her magical reserves were low again. She'd need to restore her power, but first, she needed to repair and strengthen the wards. She couldn't afford to be unprotected while recovering from her rejuvenation ritual. She was also going to need help. The sooner, the better.

The wards on her home were barely dented, so she took care of those first, but the wards surrounding the property were badly damaged. After an hour, and using nearly all of her reserves, she was able to restore and reinforce the wards that helped to keep her and her home safe.

Using precious little of her power, Suleima called two small pigeons. On one leg of each, she placed a short note. The first to the wolf Alpha, Gage: *Had a visitor when I returned home.* The second note to a close friend: *It has started again. I need your help. Wards broken by banshee. Come quickly. I must recharge.* She pushed her will into the two birds, sending them off in different directions, and watched as they flew off.

One last task was required before recharging, and it would use all of her remaining power. She stirred the air, pulling soil and leaves from the ground, showering them over her home and yard. "As it was so long ago, it shall appear again. Time stands still and comes to an end. Until I wake, it shall not be. Cloaked from all, it can't be seen."

Her legs felt wobbly as she walked into the cabin to begin her ritual. She hoped her friend got her message, because she couldn't wait for help to arrive. Her eyes began drooping as the sparks from the ritual rained down over her, though these were bright enough to light up her yard through the small windows of her cabin.

She barely made it to the bed before collapsing.

It was nearly dinnertime the next day when she woke. Suleima breathed a sigh of relief at the familiar presence above her. She walked out onto her porch. A small push of will, and the cloaking spell which hid her home dissolved in a rain of tiny sparkles. A few steps off her porch, she turned to look on the roof, smiling. "So glad to see you, Dyna. I have missed you, but I am sorry this brings us together again."

The large, royal blue dragon stretched, each scale clicking as the muscles beneath moved. She then launched herself from the roof, transforming in midair to land in front of Suleima in human form—a tall, curvy woman with hair the color of her scales and bright blue, smiling eyes. She hugged Suleima. "It has been too long." Her tone grew serious. "How bad is it this time?"

"We have some time, I think, to prepare. Last night was the first attack at my home, but when the banshee fails to return, they will be sure I am here. He's been trying to find me, and now he is going to know that he has." Suleima led the way into her cabin and started a fire with a push of will in the stove to make tea and dinner. "I've been in contact with the Amber Mountain Pack. They are willing to help us. I will need your help to find out the strength of Dirrin's forces."

"I've already sent three scouts. I should be hearing from them soon," Dynasira said, sitting down at the small table next to the kitchen.

Suleima filled the teapot from the old pump at the sink, but it clattered to the floor, and she dashed for the door of her cabin.

Dynasira sniffed as she exited the cabin behind her. "Wolves."

"The Amber Mountain Pack." Suleima gestured for Dynasira to stay where she was and walked past the perimeter of her wards, just as the first wolf emerged with its teeth bared. The gray-and-black coat of the Alpha stood on end. He eyed Dynasira but stopped directly in front of Suleima. She could sense the many wolves scattered around her home, but could only see three; the Alpha, a wolf with a red coat, nearly as large as the Alpha, and a smaller, sand-colored wolf, the one from the orc attack, standing just behind it. She sensed Kaly, coming on foot from the dirt road where she'd left her truck, so she stood silently and waited.

Kaly was barely in sight when she started speaking, presumably translating for the Alpha. "Who is the creature? And why is it in our territory?"

"The creature? You mean my friend. Dynasira, a dragon from the Azula clan. She came at my request. The incident from last night left my power drained lower than I could afford, and I needed help as quickly as possible. She fought beside me in the battles in Setura. Her help is invaluable, and she is in *my* territory, Alpha." Suleima directed her answer to the gray wolf.

The Alpha snarled at Suleima, causing Kaly to shrink back slightly. She felt Dynasira step off the porch and raised a hand to stall her friend. A battle did not need to start right now.

A slight nod from the Alpha and Kaly spoke again. "We were out on a hunt when your bird arrived. When we returned this afternoon, Gage was needed to handle an incident within the pack, so Wade,"—she gestured to the red wolf—"the Pack's second, was sent here to check on you. Your cabin was gone. As well as any scent trace of you."

"A temporary cloaking spell. I needed to recharge my powers, which would leave me essentially unconscious for several hours. I couldn't risk anyone finding me without any protection," she explained.

Gage's wolf visibly settled. "We will need to meet again to develop a plan," Kaly stated.

"I will have more information soon." Suleima looked back to her friend who gestured. "In about two hours. We can meet you in three."

Kaly looked startled, and then spoke, "Your friend, if you insist she be present, must be in human form."

"She poses no threat to you or yours; of this you have my word," Suleima stated. "But in the interest of our friendship, I feel I should make you aware; she does not require the time it takes you to change." She turned to Dynasira and pointed to the roof of her cabin. Dynasira nodded, took a few steps, and leapt into the air, landing on the roof in full dragon form.

She felt the shock of the wolves before she turned around. "I see dragons are new to you. Most of them are on our side, working against Dirrin and his army."

Dynasira jumped back into the air and let out a loud warning screech. The wolves bristled, baring their teeth at the dragon.

Suleima sensed it then. She pulled violently at the air, concentrating it near the ground, so as not to throw off Dynasira's flight. The wolves snarled and fought against the wind as they tried to face off with the dragon. Then Gage aimed his snarls at her. Kaly had wrapped herself around a tree to keep from being blown around.

Dynasira slammed an object onto the ground between Suleima and Gage with her clawed feet. The broken creature lay on its back, death clouding its eyes. A gargoyle. Another scout. Suleima dropped her pull on the air as Dynasira approached.

Suleima stood, scanning with all of her senses and abilities for anything else out of the ordinary. Finding nothing, she gestured to Dynasira, who landed next to her as a human.

"I apologize, Alpha, for startling you. My aggression was a warning," Dynasira stated matter-of-factly.

Gage nodded stiffly.

Suleima walked toward the remains of the gargoyle. Its teeth, pointed and sharp, were visible in the sneer on its face as it died. Its leathery, snow-white skin was burned on one side, bright red scars marring it and having melted the left ear away. Suleima momentarily closed her eyes at the sight.

Dynasira closed the gap between them, gently placing her hand on Suleima's left shoulder. "He won't get away with this again. We will stop him this time." Suleima nodded, and Dynasira dropped her hand.

Suleima shook herself out of her musings. Something was off. She opened her senses and liquefied the ground to her left before snapping it solid again, trapping the legs of the black wolf sneaking in on her flank. The three wolves, the same aggressive ones from the first meeting with the wolves, growled and snapped their jaws.

When Dynasira took a step toward them, Gage growled, but placed himself between his wolves and Suleima again.

Kaly's eyes snapped to Gage, but she spoke to Suleima. "Release them, please."

Reluctantly, Suleima released them, but she held her power close.

The black wolf lunged at her, but Gage had him by the throat and pinned to the ground in the blink of the eye.

"Asher, you and your friends will go back to the pack house with Wade, now." Kaly's voice was calm, almost quiet, but held the power of the Alpha within it. Asher whined pitifully, and the wolves with him dropped to the ground.

The red wolf approached and bared his teeth. They stood, their heads lowered and cocked to the side, exposing their necks. Gage gave a last warning shake to Asher's neck before releasing him. When Asher's wolf gave a last sneer in her direction, Gage snapped his teeth over Asher's nose.

"You won't be told again, Asher." Kaly's voice still held the Alpha's power.

The wolves slunk away, the red wolf right behind, making sure they went where they were ordered to.

"I apologize, Alpha, for startling you. There was no time to warn you, or I would have done so. Gargoyles are fast. Dirrin uses them as scouts. Having seen all of us together, we could not allow it to get back to Dirrin," Dynasira said.

"With three of his minions now missing, that is enough confirmation for him that I am here. He will assume that I have come to you for help. Your pack could be another target now. I'm sorry."

"The attacks are coming far faster than I had ever thought they would." Kaly said, "We will meet at the pack house. Today." The command of the Alpha was clear in her voice.

"Gage, Dirrin has a distinct signature to his work. The burns. His primary power is fire. He's done a lot of damage to supernaturals and humans alike with his powers. He enjoys the marks it leaves." Suleima gestured to the body of the gargoyle. "This unnatural was an ally. He does worse to those who oppose him. I tell you this because you need to know and understand what you are up against. Joining us in this battle will put you and your pack in grave danger."

"We are already involved, Suleima," Kaly replied for him. "We get the danger."

"I don't think you do, Alpha." Dynasira stepped forward, "Pack Setura stayed out of the fight last time. The few wolves we managed to recruit were rogues. None survived. There is a chance no one survives against Dirrin. There are those of us who are willing to risk it all to stop him. You have to be willing to do so as well, to sacrifice your entire pack, or we don't want your help."

Gage bristled, and Suleima placed herself between the Alpha wolf and Dynasira. "There are serious consequences to facing off with Dirrin. Death is sometimes the easiest to deal with." Suleima looked up to the sky, raised her hands above her head, and wiped them down her face, to reveal an angry scar along the entire left side. The glamor lifted completely, showing a left hand damaged beyond repair, wrinkled welts covering the whole of it. "He shows no mercy and burns without thought. He nearly killed me the last time, and he left me with a lifetime of pain." In a flash, she replaced her glamor.

The shock on the faces in front of her was enough to deal with, but the pity in their eyes was just too much. She turned and walked back into her cabin. Suleima was tired of the fight, tired of the constant worry.

She wanted to bring the fight to him, not just wait for attacks, but she needed to be smart. She couldn't run headlong into this battle.

It would put everyone at risk. She needed to get him one-on-one and keep everyone else out of danger.

Chapter 4

"She doesn't show those scars lightly, Alpha. I'm a friend, and I've never seen the full extent of them. She shows you, so you know what could happen to your pack. She knows some fates are worse than death. Living with the constant reminder of a failure which killed so many others. A battle destined to repeat itself. Suleima felt every loss on our side. She holds those losses within herself. She holds herself responsible and will not rest until she knows she has done all she can to rectify those deaths." Dynasira turned away. "I was the one who found her that night. She begged me to let her die. I did not. I could not.

"She is the only one who can take on Dirrin. He is protected by spells I cannot touch. Spells you won't be able to touch. All we can do is support her in this journey. We need you to understand this is a battle unlike any other you have fought."

Gage turned away. There was no question in his mind about joining this fight. The only question was whether or not to allow his wolves to take part. They needed to meet, before another meeting with Suleima and this dragon friend of hers. His wolves were his responsibility, and he wouldn't force them to participate. Those scars on Suleima were no small thing, and although wolves healed quickly, Kaly was proof there could still be consequences from an injury like that. He shifted and changed into clothes he kept in Kaly's car.

Kaly approached Gage with caution, likely sensing the conflict within him. She had such a special bond with him and with Wade since the injury, which left her scarred. A challenge because of Kaly's dominance. The other wolf could not handle the fact that a woman was more dominant than him. The sneak attack wounded more than just her throat. But Kaly was slowly coming back to herself, and to assert her dominance again, more and more. "I want to fight with her. Alongside you."

"It is dangerous, Kaly. You saw the scars. You are still healing."

"I need to fight alongside her, Gage. It is important to me. To my healing." Kaly was holding back, and Gage knew it. She was afraid of overstepping. Although the wolf who attacked her was no longer a part of their pack, he still had friends there. Friends who felt the same way about a dominant female.

"I won't stop you from fighting, Kaly. It is your decision."

Kaly walked with Gage back to the cabin. As he approached, he could see sparks of varying colors dropping from the ceiling through the window. He watched, fascinated, as she spun in the middle of the room, catching those sparks as they drifted down. When she stopped and bowed her head, he knocked lightly on the door.

"We need to head back down the mountain. I need to meet with my wolves," he stated simply, as she opened the door.

"I want to apologize. I didn't intend to reveal my scars, but seeing them on the gargoyle who was working for him . . . I wanted to make sure you knew exactly what danger you and your wolves could be in."

"No need to apologize. I cannot imagine how difficult it has been for you. You will have Kaly and I in battle with you. The rest of my wolves will need to make that choice for themselves. I will not force them into this battle. They must participate willingly."

"I thank you for any help you are able to give."

Chapter 5

Time would not be on their side. Dynasira would return soon—she had left to find out what she could about Dirrin's forces—and they would head to the Pack's house.

Suleima sent out messages to as many of her allies from before as she could. Many of them had headed west, as she had, to heal after the last battle, some just to hide. They needed to know what numbers they had to work with. But she also needed to figure out how to handle it all without jeopardizing the lives of every being in this war.

Her birds returned with their messages. Some allies were willing to fight, others were still too traumatized by the last one. Suleima understood. If there was any way for her to bow out, to hide, to disappear, she would. But there would be no backing down this time. She would give her life. She would sacrifice everything to defeat him. She would succeed, or she would die trying. There was no other option. One way or another, this would be the last battle between her and Dirrin.

Sensing Dynasira's return, Suleima met her out on the porch. "He's gathered nearly as many minions as before. He's recruited several necromancers, more powerful than those that he had before. They have revived several of the dangerous beasts we were able to defeat last time. They are back, they are undead. They will be much more dangerous and much harder to kill. They are moving slowly in this direction. We have a couple months before he gets here. With a group that size, they are moving mostly at night. He doesn't seem to want to call attention to himself this time. And he isn't targeting cities. It seems that *you* are his first step.

"Our numbers have dwindled, as we expected. Most of the Dragon Clans will send who they can, some are more willing than others. Clan Schwara is with Dirrin. The death dragons have not changed their position. They are still stupid enough to believe he will share his power and not try to rule over them, if he reaches his goal."

"Thank you, Dyna." Suleima returned to the house and began gathering items to make some tea.

Once they were seated, Suleima continued, "We will be short on help, as we were before. We can't battle his army one-on-one. I am unwilling to resort to the magic he is using. Although the power could help us, it would make us no better than him. I'll consult the few books I was able to save of Erist's, but I have yet to find much that could help us."

"Have you kept up with your Ritual of Alucenia?" she asked.

"I completed it right after the gargoyle appeared, and I'll do so again before we head to the pack house. I must be at full power to fight Dirrin. He is too strong now, Dyna. I'm not sure I can defeat him."

"I will do everything I can to help you, Suleima. I know that you can defeat him. You won't be alone. We can't allow him to win. Not this time. I feel our next meeting with him will be the final meeting, one way or another."

"On that, we certainly agree. Our timing and strategy must be perfect, or we will be leading many to their deaths, including ourselves." Suleima stood, gulping down the remainder of her tea. "I'll complete my ritual and meet you in the yard. Then we will head to the pack house together."

"You going to make me ride in that deathtrap of a vehicle you drive?"

"You heard Gage. You must be in human form in his territory."

"He's no fun!"

Suleima grinned, gathering her ingredients. "I think he is new to most of this. He's had his wolves, but one of the many reasons I chose to come here, is the lack of others. He hasn't had exposure to the variety and types of beings we have encountered in Setura."

"He'll be in for a huge surprise then." Dynasira left, closing the door behind her, leaving Suleima alone to complete her ritual.

Suleima found it difficult to clear her mind to begin the ritual. She was worried about so many things. Taking a deep breath, she calmed her mind as best as she could. There was a spark of an idea, but it was gone before she could grasp it. Suleima sat, putting aside the renewal ritual, closed her eyes, and drew in a deep breath. If she could just clear her mind, she could find that spark again. She closed her eyes, going in her mind to the most peaceful place she could think of—the meadow half a mile from her home—and felt her whole body slowly relax, muscle by muscle.

She stood suddenly and walked to her cabinet, throwing the doors open wide and grabbing an old, damaged book. She flipped through it and found what caused the spark.

The spell would need to be translated, but this could be exactly what she needed. Quickly cloaking the book, she put it back in the cabinet and left with Dynasira.

Driving with Dynasira was an experience. She gripped the door handle and dashboard with all her might and left a handprint dent in the dash. She sucked her breath in through her teeth at every turn and slammed her eyes shut on the descent of every hill.

When they pulled into the long driveway which led up to the house, Suleima scanned the property. There were far fewer wolves than at her first visit. She felt the presence of many of them, just on the outskirts of the property, keeping watch. Kaly and Gage were inside, along with about ten other wolves.

Suleima parked the car. Dynasira jumped out before the car came to a full stop. "I hope that's not a commentary on my driving." Suleima smiled at her as she got out herself.

"I don't know how you do it all the time! I am perfectly capable of flying wherever I want to go."

Kaly was waiting on the front porch to greet them. She opened the door, allowing them to precede her into the house. Gage was just inside.

"Welcome back, Suleima. Welcome, Dynasira." Gage led them into the same large room where Suleima had first addressed the pack. "To begin with, we are down quite a few of my wolves. Thirty or so have agreed to participate. All of them are strong fighters. I've asked my second, Wade, to stay out of the fight. In the event something happens to me, I want the remainder of my pack to still have a strong leader."

"We have the help of several Dragon Clans. There are a few shamans left. They aren't willing to face Dirrin in battle again, but they will be able to help with healings. Pack Setura will not be sending any of their wolves, but I never thought they would. There are a few jinn on our side, but their magic is not meant to damage others. They, again, are helpful with healing and cloaking spells or misdirection. There will also be a group of thunderbirds. But I will be honest with you, we are very outnumbered." Suleima continued before Gage could interrupt, "Dirrin has necromancers, lich, giants, and orcs, just to name a few. He has used gargoyles, like the one we encountered earlier today, posting them in places not easily seen, to alert him of oncoming attackers, making it difficult to sneak up on him. His necromancers have brought back some of the creatures we defeated in the past. The jinn may be able to disrupt the necromancers' spells, but I'm not positive about that, yet."

"The Jorogumo is one of the creatures he's brought back. It's an enormous, venomous spider that can change into a harmless-appearing woman. She was able to take out several wolves who fought with us last time.

"A cyclops, and at least one ent, are also rumored to have been brought back. Their sheer size makes them extremely difficult to take down. The ents had been corrupted by Dirrin's mentor in black magics, otherwise, I doubt they would have even chosen a side, let alone fight for Dirrin," Dynasira added.

"This keeps getting better and better," one of the wolves muttered.

"You are all volunteers. If you don't like what you are hearing, shut it and bow out, Asher." Gage pointedly looked at the wolf who'd spoken, one of the same wolves who had interrupted Suleima on her first trip to the pack house. "This will be dangerous. But I for one would rather die in this battle than be forced to bow down to this Dirrin person. If you don't agree, you've seen the door. Use it. There is no room for waffling. This goes for all of you, either you fight with us, fully, or you stay the hell home and out of our way." The wolf who had spoken out of turn shifted uncomfortably under Gage's glare. None of the other wolves moved a muscle.

"We will have to come up with a strategic plan to hit them, because we are far outnumbered. Taking them head-on would be a fatal mistake." Dynasira scanned the room as she spoke. "We have just about two months before he arrives, if he stays at his current pace. It is obvious Dirrin is trying to weaken Suleima because he is afraid of her. She is the only one strong enough to defeat him."

"He's not afraid of me. He believes he is powerful enough now to beat me. He nearly did the last time we faced off."

Suleima had something she wanted to speak with Gage and Dynasira about. She wasn't ready to share it with the entire pack yet. Not until she had more. "May we speak privately?"

Gage nodded and dismissed his wolves, sending them out to increase the perimeter guard. He led Suleima and Dynasira down a flight of stairs to a lower level and closed a heavy steel door. "This room is designed to hold a werewolf who has lost control. It is designed so no sound will escape the room. Whatever is shared in this room, you can believe it will not be heard by anyone."

"There is something Dirrin doesn't know. Before retreating here, I managed to make it back to what remained of Erist's home, one last time. It had been years since I'd set foot on the property. This time, I was able to find a book that had been hidden beneath the floorboards. They must have been protected by one of Erist's spells. I've found a spell I may be able to use to even the playing field, but part of the spell was charred, and I must piece it together. It is a complicated spell, and if I don't get it exactly right, it will be a deadly mistake."

"What do you need to complete the spell?" Gage asked.

"I'm not sure yet. It is a very old book. The pages are extremely faded, on top of the charring. It is written in the Old World Tongue, so I will have to translate it. Part of what I need to translate is the ingredients I need to gather to prep the spell. And then the spell itself. And I'm not sure how I would pull it off, but I may need to find someone to use as a guinea pig. If I can find a person who fits the requirements and test the spell, at least I would know I could make the spell work, once I got close. Somehow, I doubt I will have people lining up to volunteer for that position."

"We could capture, instead of kill, one of these creatures Dirrin is sending to try to weaken you," Dynasira offered.

"It can't be a demon or banshee. It must be a magic wielder. Specifically, a magic wielder who has worked in the black magics. I believe this spell is designed to take away the power gained by performing black magics. Dirrin has done so much, sacrificed so many in the name of gaining power from their deaths. It is why he is so strong. If I can pull that power away, return it to the elements, we would be evenly matched.

He's surrounded himself with beings who are dangerous but not magic wielders. The only possibilities would be the lich or necromancers. I'm not sure it would work on the lich, because they are already dead and brought back by those necromancers. The necromancers will send their minions rather than face us themselves. Getting a guinea pig could be almost as difficult as getting to Dirrin."

"Does he know you have this spell?" Gage asked. "Could he counter it if he knew?"

"I would guess he doesn't know of its existence, but I can't be sure. It was only a spark of a memory that made me look for it, a story Erist told me long ago. I'm not sure what even made me think of it. Dirrin did destroy Erist's books after killing him. But I don't know if he was doing that to destroy a specific spell. He was so angry with Erist. And me. I'd always excelled in magic. It always came quicker to me. He created a rivalry between us, which I didn't realize existed.

"So could he counter it? It would have to be the perfect spell, specifically designed to counter it, and he would have to know about the spell to do it. In theory, yes. But, Dirrin was never really successful with intricate spells. He's more of a smash-it-with-a-hammer guy. It is possible, but not likely. It's all a risk."

Suleima and Dynasira stood to leave, "I'll return tomorrow to strengthen the wards surrounding the property. I'll come in the afternoon. It will not be as hard on the wolves as when it was put in place, but it will not be comfortable for them either."

"Kaly will be here; I'll make sure most of the other wolves are out of range."

The three of them walked out to the yard. Only a few wolves remained in the area.

"One more thing..." Dynasira bowed her head slightly. "May I fly out of here?"

Suleima hid her grin as best as she could. Dynasira wasn't a person to capitulate to anyone, let alone an Alpha. She must really not want to get back in the car.

The instant Gage nodded, Dynasira was in the air.

Once she returned home, Suleima performed her Ritual of Alucenia and then uncloaked the spell book. She was determined to find something, anything, in the book that would help her complete the spell. Using some of her own spell books, she was able to translate a few of the words from the Old World text, but she needed to find a more comprehensive book to help with translating.

She closed her eyes, opening her sight, hoping by looking at the book with all of her senses, it would bring something new to light. She scanned the page with no hint of a clue. She sighed heavily, pushing out her will, asking the elements for guidance. The window blew open, air rushing in and flipping the pages of the book to another spell.

Shocked at the suddenness, Suleima backed away from the table. She saw nothing out of the ordinary on the page. She dropped the magic she held, and just opened her eyes.

This spell was also in the Old World Tongue.

How would this help? Frustrated, she slammed her hand on the table, knocking one of her other books onto the floor. As she picked it up, it seemed to vibrate. She placed it onto the table and rested a hand on top.

She sat back down and looked again at the Old World Tongue spell. Something about it seemed familiar. She was able to pick out a couple words that seemed familiar and were in the other spell. A few she had been able to translate, but most of them she couldn't.

Her eyes were tired, and her mind was in a jumble.

Suleima went for a walk to clear her head. She walked along a small creek bed, the water singing to her senses. She closed her eyes, allowing the movement of the water to clear her mind, wash away the knots in her head. Parting the canopy of the trees, she basked in the sunlight that streamed through, the slight breeze that ruffled her hair.

She stayed there a while, surrounding herself with the elements, flexing her power with each of the elements in turn, feeling her connection to them.

Something kept trying to click in her mind about the spell that she was trying to translate, as she walked and bathed in the nature surrounding her home, but every time she reached for it, it slipped away, leaving her no closer and continually frustrated.

Suleima woke with a start. It was just dawn outside. Opening her senses, a quick scan told her all was well currently with her wards. She could feel Dynasira off in the distance, in the place she had been sleeping. Suleima jumped from the bed, tossed a log on the hot coals, reignited the stove with a push of will, and placed her kettle on top. Then she sat at the spell book, staring at it, dumbfounded. She knew this spell, knew it by heart. It was a spell she had performed thousands of times. It was the Ritual of Alucenia.

She wrote out the spell as she knew it and compared the words to those in the Old World Tongue. Each of the words she knew in the Old World Tongue matched up perfectly. Each of the others seemed to work. The ingredients were the same. She wrote down the Old World words above her spell, then flipped to the new spell. She was able to decipher most of the spell between what she had already translated and her new epiphany. She only had a handful of words left to translate, but she was able to see the one ingredient she knew would be a trial to get: the Flame of the Truest Heart.

Erist had told tales of the great adventure, taken with his mentor, to find a very rare flower which held much mystical power. High above the clouds in a mountain, deep within a cave. The trail, according to Erist's stories, was fraught with dangerous creatures who rarely ventured off the mountain. This flower was going to be insanely difficult to retrieve, but it was the *only* thing that could make this spell work. The only way to get to the top of the mountain was to climb. There were no shortcuts, like sending a dragon, or even riding one. It would be a hike with tests along the way. It is the only story she remembered Erist telling about his mentor. They took the trek together, Erist's mentor being the one who completed the challenges, but she couldn't remember any stories about his mentor before or after that trial.

Suleima called forth two pigeons and sent messages to Dynasira and Gage to meet her at the cabin. Then she started to prepare.

She packed a bedroll, a few changes of clothes, ropes, foodstuffs, and canteens. She also packed up her main spell book and the book with the spell she intended to use on Dirrin. It would likely be too difficult of a journey and too dark for her to work on the translation while she was gone, but she couldn't leave it behind. If Dirrin or his forces were able to break through her protections and find it, this would have all been for naught. Finally, she added the items needed to perform the Ritual of Alucenia daily. She rolled it all up into her tent and tied on straps. As she was finishing, she sensed Gage approaching, Dynasira right behind him.

She opened the door and headed out to meet them, pushing against her wards to allow Gage to enter.

"I need to go away for a while. I'll be gone a few weeks at minimum. While I'm gone, I'm going to place a spell on my cabin to make it appear abandoned. I would like to put a similar spell on the pack house. My hope is that any unnaturals who show up while I am gone will think that we have all run."

"Where will you be going?" Dyna asked.

"I've figured out most of the spell. There is an ingredient I need, a very rare flower. I need to travel to Mount Lucent, to a hidden cave near the summit. "

"I'll fly you up to the peak," Dynasira said.

"While I appreciate the offer, it is forbidden. There are magical properties surrounding the mountain, and they won't allow it. I must pass challenges to reach the flower. Erist accompanied his mentor as a rite of passage. Had Dirrin not killed him, I imagine it is a trip Erist and I would have taken together at some point."

"Who will be accompanying you?" Gage asked.

"I'll travel alone."

"No, you won't. You will need to sleep at some point. You have no idea what you will run into. You need to have someone with you."

"I need Dyna to stay here. She needs to be able to help if the spells don't deter Dirrin's minions. I also need her to coordinate with the other Dragon Clans, so when I do return, we can be ready to face Dirrin with all we've got."

"I'll leave Wade in charge of the pack. You cannot do this alone. The rumors of Mount Lucent are legendary. I'll go with you and help keep watch when you can't."

"I appreciate the offer, but . . ."

"No buts. You don't go alone," Dynasira interrupted. "Gage has offered to go with you, and if I can't go, then he needs to."

"I can't ask you to do that, Gage. Leaving your pack behind without an Alpha? With this threat looming, it is too much to ask."

"You aren't asking. I have offered. We have no idea what you will encounter. I can't risk sending another of my pack with you. I will not risk them. Wade is more than capable of handling the pack and any issues that arise until I return." Gage left no room for argument in his tone.

Dynasira jumped back into the argument. "This is not meant to be a journey taken alone. Erist accompanied his mentor and would have taken you on the journey himself."

Suleima sighed, knowing she would never win the argument. "Fine."

Before heading out of the woods, Suleima performed the spell to make her home look abandoned. She cringed slightly as she weakened the wards, so it would look like they were fading from lack of care and upkeep.

The three of them headed down the mountain to the pack house.

Wade and Kaly were at the house when they arrived. Gage met with them to fill them in, while Suleima went out to prepare the spell. She weakened the wards first. She was grateful there were only a couple of wolves at the house. It was always unpredictable, how they would react to the use of magic. Erist had never really explained why spells could be cast in a battle and not affect the wolves at all, but putting up wards and protection spells could be so painful for them.

Once the wards were weakened, she headed back to the house. Gage was on the porch looking aggravated. "Everything OK?"

"Several of my wolves aren't responding to attempts to contact them." Gage hung his head. "It's the wolves who have been a problem, Asher and his group of friends. I can't decide if it is a good thing or a bad thing. They have been a problem since they joined, and even more so since Kaly was attacked by their buddy."

"I am sorry if I have brought yet another problem to your door."

"I'm wondering if you could include those wolves in the spell, so they are unable to see if anyone is here. At least while I'm away. Until we have some answers."

"I'll need something of theirs. Do they keep anything here? Clothes or grooming items that only they use?"

"They each have a locker just outside the safe room downstairs. They usually keep extra clothes and stuff in there. I'll bring you something from each of them. They have the ability to contact Wade, in the event they do come back and find everyone gone."

Gage left Suleima on the porch, in search of the objects she needed. Kaly stepped out onto the porch. "Gage is leaving with you? How long will you be gone?"

"Yes, apparently. I'm not sure how long we will be gone. A couple weeks, I would think. These spells will last at least that long. I need to be sure, both for myself and for Gage, that you and the rest of the pack will be safe in our absence."

"I appreciate it, Suleima. Please keep Gage safe in your travels. I'm sure it will not be an easy trek."

"I'll do everything in my power to bring him back to you."

"We have been connected since after my attack, since my recovery. I don't know what I would do without him. He has kept me safe." She seemed so small and timid as she spoke.

"You have a strength I envy, Kaly. You are stronger than you realize."

"I don't think so."

"Even so, I sense a strength and courage in you, even if you don't. You have been able to remain a strong member of this pack, holding your own against a group of wolves who you know have been hostile to you since you were attacked by their friend. I believe you will surprise yourself before this is all said and done."

Gage came out of the house with items for each of the missing wolves.

"This spell will be a rough one to stand through. Would you rather clear out?"

"No, go ahead." Wade came out onto the porch with Gage and Kaly.

Suleima sat on the ground and gathered the items around her. "Only pack members, except these three will be able to see through the glamour around the house. Everyone else will see the house as having been abandoned."

She closed her eyes and let out a soft hum. Concentrating on the items and property, Suleima set the spell in place and sealed it tight, doing her best to ignore the grinding of teeth and muffled groans coming from the three wolves just feet from her.

When she completed the spell, Suleima stood up. "Could I have a glass of water please?" Gage nodded at Wade, who went into the house to get it.

"I see nothing different," Gage stated. "But lord, that spell hurt."

"As the pack leader, you will see no difference. For the rest of your wolves, there will be a fuzziness around the house. Some will see more than others."

"I see it." Kaly interjected. "The door seems to almost be vibrating."

"To anyone else the house will appear abandoned. If I cloaked the house, anyone who knew it was here would know it was under a spell and could eventually break through. This way, hopefully, anyone we don't want here will think we have all run to hide. Dirrin knows how badly I was injured."

"Although the idea of hiding doesn't sit well with me, I also want to prevent as many attacks as possible while we are away." Gage turned and headed back into the house, as Wade brought out the glass of water.

Suleima thanked him for the water and headed with her pack of supplies to the middle of the front yard. She pulled out the ingredients she would need to recharge and began the ritual. Kaly had ventured off the porch and stood watching. "You can come a bit closer if you would like. Just give me a ten-foot radius or so. The light show is pretty."

By the time she finished spinning under the sparks, she had an audience of three wolves and a dragon.

"That's amazing," Kaly said in awe. "If you don't mind my asking, how does that all work?"

Suleima smiled shyly, "I use the smallest bit of my power to call to each of the elements and ask them to refill my power. There is a finite amount that I am able to carry and to use at any particular time. The sparks that rain down from the orbs are representative of the energies pouring in to fill up my power 'well.'"

"What happens if you run yourself completely dry of power?" Gage asked.

"Because of my talents with the elements, I have, I guess you could call it a drop of power, that will never run out. I would never be able to use that to cast any sort of spell, but I can use it to call to the elements to refill my power."

"What happens if the elements refuse?" Kaly asked.

"I... I don't know,' Suleima answered thoughtfully. "I've never had that happen."

"I know I'll never get tired of watching that light show," Dynasira stated before walking forward. "I did a quick flight around. I'm not seeing anything out of the ordinary. I also found a place about halfway between here and your cabin where I will be able to set up a place to nest and sleep." She turned to Kaly and Wade. "I'll be nearby if there is any problem. Give a shout or a howl, and I'll be here as fast as I can."

Wade nodded before turning to Gage. "I've got this. You go get whatever it is she needs. We need every advantage we can, especially now that we are down more wolves."

"We may be able to send word to you at least through part of the journey. Anything you need to communicate to Gage can be sent back on the same bird I send to you."

Gage wished them luck, grabbed his own pack, and headed out to his car.

"We'll need a truck." Suleima said. "You are welcome to drive, but we will take my truck." She nodded to Dynasira before following Gage. "Keep them safe."

Chapter 6

THEY WERE AN HOUR into the trip when Gage finally spoke. "Thank you for what you said to Kaly. She has struggled so much since the attack she suffered."

"I truly believe she is so much stronger than she realizes. I would not have said anything otherwise. You two share such a special connection—I think she feels like her courage all comes from you."

"She is a dominant wolf. Some of the older males resent that. The one who attacked her did not challenge her; he blindsided her. A sneak attack. He nearly tore her throat out. You've seen the scars. She somehow managed to get away from him before he could finish the job, and she turned the tables on him, despite what should have been a fatal injury. She gave back nearly as good as she got. Opened up three of his four legs and got him on his back. She couldn't get him by his neck, so she opened up his gut. That's when I found them. I separated them, forced their shift. Kaly obviously wasn't able to tell me what happened, but the security cameras did. The wolf took off before I could kill him, despite protests from his friends, the wolves who have currently gone missing. Kaly's healing took a long time. We think he went to some sort of a magic wielder, someone willing to do black magic. Whatever it was, her wounds wouldn't heal. She and I somehow developed a kind of psychic connection, so we could communicate while she was unable to speak. I'm still not sure how it all came about."

"I will look into my spell books to see if anything can be done about her injury, to see if it can be healed now. But, because it was so long ago, I doubt it."

"She's fine with how it is now. And, as you said, she is stronger than she realizes. That girl is going to make some man miserable someday. She's been with us since this pack was formed. When I left my old pack to begin this one, she was coming into her own and showing just how dominant she might become. That pack leader was one of those who thought the woman's place in the pack was below all of the males. They were beginning to bully her and treat her badly, no matter her form. I didn't like it, and neither did my wolf. She came with me. We have a connection I can't describe. My wolf adopted her as my own; she is my daughter now." He sat quiet for a few moments before speaking again, "I'm not sure why I keep talking around you. It's not something that is usual for me. Other than giving orders, I am usually quiet. Even with Kaly, there isn't a lot of chatting."

They traveled for several more hours before stopping for a quick dinner along the side of the road. They switched drivers and continued on through the night. They were making good time, on track to reach the base of the mountain by dinnertime the following day. Gage's breathing evened out, and Suleima knew he was sleeping.

She stared out the windshield.

The fight to survive and heal after the last battle with Dirrin was difficult, but if she failed at this, many more would die. If she floundered in her effort to get this flower, or if the spell didn't work . . . she was running out of ideas on how to even face Dirrin, let alone defeat him. The weight she felt on her shoulders was crushing. How was it she, of all the people in the world, ended up the one to face this?

She sensed the deer before it came into the road, allowing her to slow down ahead of time, so as to not disturb Gage's sleep.

She felt a calmness with him that did not come easily to her, at least not in many, many years. She could sit in a peaceful silence with him, or talk, and she felt equally as comfortable. The fact that he stood up against his original pack for a female wolf was a statement of his character: he would not allow those weaker to suffer at the hands of another.

Pack Setura was the complete opposite.

The Alpha of Setura hadn't hesitated to refuse involvement when he was approached before the battle. They were content to sit by and watch innocent people hurt and be killed.

Gage was so very different.

Gage drove the final leg of the journey, switching with her near dawn. She did her best to rest her eyes and prepare for the challenges ahead. Erist had once explained that the challenges would be different for each person attempting to reach the flower.

She followed instinct as they approached the base of the mountain, and at the spot she indicated, Gage pulled her truck to a stop. The trees were dense, and the birds around them sang loudly. She knew the landscape would change greatly by the time they reached the top of the mountain. She could only hope she had prepared enough.

"What will we face?" Gage asked, throwing his pack onto his shoulder as they started up the trail.

"I will be challenged in each of the four elements. I'm not sure of the order, or what the challenges will be." She walked in silence for a bit before speaking again. "These will be dangerous challenges, Gage."

"I have faced challenges before. I can handle myself."

"But these are not *your* challenges. They are mine. You cannot lead the fight here. You cannot be Alpha. Can you do that?"

"Alpha is not something I can turn off and on. It is my duty to protect those around me," Gage answered.

"I need your word you will allow me to do what I need to do. You cannot interfere in any way. There will be consequences if you do. I need you to follow my lead."

"I'll do my best. That is all I can promise you."

Suleima nodded before heading further into the woods. "It's already getting dark. We should stop for the night. We have had a long drive, and I'd prefer to be rested when the first challenge is presented. There is a small outcropping of rocks just ahead, about a hundred yards from the trail. We can set up camp there. We should be able to see anything coming at us, and we'll be protected from behind."

Gage led the way, despite Suleima's earlier warnings.

They set up the tents as a large tarp, covering the outcropping, then covered it with leaves, to conceal the shelter. Companionably, they walked around the area, gathering sticks and logs to use for firewood. When the collection was big enough to last the night, Suleima sat next to the pit they created and pulled at her power with fire, causing a spark. Nurturing it with air, the dry twigs and leaves quickly caught, and the fire was roaring within minutes.

Gage shifted to hunt down some dinner, while Suleima grabbed some edible plants that grew within sight of the camp. He shook out his fur, and Suleima reached out with her senses. There were a few animals just to the west of their camp and she sent Gage in that direction, letting his nose do the rest.

While he hunted, Suleima walked the short distance to a small creek that she felt. She pulled out one of the canteens. Closing her eyes and breathing deeply, Suleima pulled at her power over water and earth, separating the impurities from the water and leaving only fresh, clean water in the canteen.

Gage returned with dinner, and she cleaned and prepared the meat for the fire. They ate a companionable dinner and settled in to take shifts and rest for the evening. Suleima set up a small warning ward about a hundred feet from their camp.

Luckily, the night was uneventful.

The next morning, they were quiet as they packed up camp and pre-pared to hike for the day. They'd both slept comfortably, as Suleima had used her power over earth to smooth and soften the ground they laid on.

She made sure now that the campsite was returned to the exact condition it was in before they had settled in for the night. Marring the pristine landscape would be a crime in itself, but neither did she want to leave a trail that someone could follow, if somehow Dirrin managed to track her here.

The path they followed was well-defined, but they could never tell which direction it would go. It seemed to appear ahead of them with each step they took.

"This is why you can't take a shortcut to the top of the mountain. The trail is being created with each step we take. The path is different for each person who takes this journey."

She was fascinated with the twists and turns that they traversed as they walked. The trail wound around in a switchback pattern, taking them up hill for a bit and then back down. In a straight line, they would have traveled more than three times as far by the time they stopped for lunch. Suleima produced a small fire and purified some water as she pulled it from another small nearby creek, while Gage got out a bit of the leftover food from dinner the night before. She had picked berries as they walked, so there was plenty to fill them up for the remainder of the hike that day.

"I wonder what is happening back home." Gage spoke softly, almost absently, as they finished the last of their lunch.

"I believe that everyone is safe. My spells should deter any of Dirrin's minions, or at the very least, confuse them. Hopefully, they will report back that we've abandoned our homes and it will throw him off, trying to find where I've gone." She paused.

An enormous grizzly bear stood on his hind legs, sniffing the air. She never even noticed its approach. The bear was downwind from them, so Gage never caught its scent either.

Gage turned quickly, and then, seeing the bear, slowly backed toward Suleima, keeping himself between them. When he reached her, she tried to push him to the side, but he wouldn't budge.

"You can't fight a grizzly, Gage. You have no time to shift, and one wolf—even an Alpha werewolf—against bear that size . . ."

Gage pulled a knife from his waistband. While it was a nice knife, it did nothing to even the playing field.

The bear left out a deafening roar. Her ears were ringing, and she couldn't imagine the effect it had on Gage's more sensitive ears.

The bear dropped to all fours, and its muscles bunched, preparing to charge.

Suleima pulled at some branches of the trees near the bear, blocking its path, and she pushed a gust of wind at it, carrying the small remains of their lunch into its face and beyond. She softened the earth beneath its feet, making it harder to find traction for its charge. At the same time, she pulled branches from a nearby tree to herself. She quickly grabbed her pack and Gage's, leaving the rest of the food and tent where it was.

Gage's eyes grew wide as the branch wrapped around him, tugging them both off the ground and into the tree about twelve feet, their feet dangling in midair, just as the grizzly charged through the branch wall she had created below.

His head snapped in her direction. "Bears climb!"

"Even if this one wanted to, these branches are too flimsy." She gritted her teeth against the power it was taking to hold them in the air as the bear tore through the supplies still on the ground. There would be holes to repair in the tent, but at least they wouldn't have to repair any holes in each other, and their clothes and most of the essential items were safe.

The food . . .that was a problem for later.

It seemed like an hour, but it was likely just a few minutes before the bear trotted off into the woods. It was gone for a few minutes before she slowly lowered Gage and herself to the ground.

"We need to gather what isn't damaged beyond repair and get moving. I can't hold us up there again until I've recharged my power, and I don't want to do it here. As it is, the next recharge may knock me out for a couple hours."

They worked quickly and quietly to gather all of the supplies they could salvage and start moving back on the trail.

Once they were moving again, Suleima apologized. "I'm sorry. I let my guard down and didn't even realize that bear was near us. I should have been scanning for wildlife and threats."

"I didn't catch his scent anywhere on the way up here. It wasn't just your fault. We both were lax in keeping an eye out. We learned a lesson and paid the price." He stuck his finger through a hole visible in the roll of tent strapped behind his head to accentuate his point.

They set up camp a little earlier that night. Suleima noticed another rocky outcropping that they could use as a partial shelter, so they could work on repairing the tent holes. She directed Gage to a good area to hunt for dinner while she used a bit of power to get the fire going, get more water, and make their beds for the night more comfortable.

When Gage returned with more food than they would need for the next few days, Suleima helped prepare it for dinner while he changed back, and then she used a bit more of her power over fire and air to dry the excess food into jerky to replace some of the lost food stores. Hunting would get harder the further up the mountain they went, and having a stockpile of jerky could save them a lot of uncomfortable days.

She performed her ritual to recharge her powers and then immediately fell into a deep sleep.

Chapter 7

THE NEXT MORNING CAME too early. She was still exhausted by the use of so much of her magic the day before. She performed the Ritual of Alucenia again, to top off her reserves.

Suleima closed her eyes and breathed in the clean, crisp air of the morning. She let the energy of the earth and elements wash over her. She could sense the birds soaring high above. Small animals scampered nearby, and larger predators were off in the distance. She sensed Gage coming up behind her before she heard him.

"Ready to head off?"

"You are the boss up here, right?" His voice held humor.

"Damn straight." Suleima slung her pack over her shoulder and headed for the trail. They walked in companionable silence through the morning.

"We should stop to eat again soon," Gage began. "I can always run ahead and hunt for something fresh to eat."

"Maybe when we stop for camp tonight, but for now, I don't want either of us venturing off too far." She had barely finished her sentence when Suleima felt the shift. Gage had stepped in front of her, and before she could warn him, the earth below him liquefied, sucking him completely underground. Suleima dropped to her knees on the now solid ground. She sank her hands in, trying to liquefy the ground again. She pulled at her powers, trying to force the earth apart. The earth element fought her, instead of flowing through her to allow her to manipulate it to her needs. It pushed against her, creating a type of friction she had never felt before. The element felt odd to her senses, a rawness, a wildness to it which made it foreign to her.

She managed to bury her arms to her elbows and reached Gage's hand. He pulled at her, trying to pull himself up, but he was stuck fast. She could sense his desperation. Suleima tried to calm herself. She took a deep breath, releasing it slowly.

She focused all of her energy on pushing the air, in a bubble, through the earth, until it surrounded Gage. She felt his hand slightly relax. She took another deep breath to calm herself; he could at least breathe. He wouldn't suffocate. She needed to slow down. With the air bubble, she could take her time. Suleima squeezed his hand. His return squeeze brought a small smile to her face. He was not panicking. She pushed more air to him, then pulled at the earth again.

When she closed her eyes, she stood in front of a beautiful dryad, who stood tall on her four tan legs. Her green and brown torso was bare, but for a few leaves scattered over her shoulder and where her torso met her legs. The deep green of her hair was contrasted by the vibrant yellow of her eyes.

Suleima looked around her. She was in a clearing in the center of a wooded area. She could still feel Gage's hand in hers.

She had been brought into a vision.

"I am the Dryad, protector of the earth element. Why are you here?" The Dryad's voice was deep, much deeper than Suleima would have expected for a female.

"I need to find the Flame," Suleima stated.

"No one reaches the Flame."

"I must reach the Flame with my companion." Suleima needed to be very careful with her words. They could be used against her later, or to manipulate her into giving something up.

"Why is that vile creation of Volos here? Why did you bring evil to my woods?"

"He is not evil." Suleima stood her ground as she felt a pull from the Dryad, "He is Alpha. He does what he must to protect his pack and those around him."

"Leave him."

"I will not. He came on this journey to help me. I will not leave him behind. I will not leave him unprotected. He is my charge in these woods. You will release him."

"You will not get the Flame. You will not reach it with him by your side."

Suleima felt Gage squeeze her hand again. She pushed more air to him. "I will not leave him buried in the ground, Dryad."

"The earth calls to you. The earth is your power. What would you do without it?"

Suleima closed her eyes. "I would be gone without it. I am the earth."

"What would you sacrifice for it?"

"He is not mine to sacrifice. Release him."

"I will not."

"Then I will."

Suleima closed her eyes and forced herself out of the vision. She pushed at the earth, but it only pushed back. She pushed more air to Gage, over and over. She pushed and pushed, growing the bubble until it surrounded his entire body. She felt him relax further as the crushing weight of the earth was no longer a strain on his body. Next, she pulled on the water within the earth. She felt it swirl around the bubble of air. Felt the sleeve of her shirt dampen. She pulled at the water below, up to her. Gage's hand emerged with hers. She gripped it even tighter and continued her pull on the water. Inch by inch, he emerged from the ground. Finally, collapsing to his knees and rolling away from the spot where he sank into the dirt.

Suleima rolled to her back, drained and out of breath. He was safe.

She barely had time to take a breath.

Her earth magic was being pulled from her. It was as if she had just used a spell which consumed all of her power. The power was there, and then it flowed out. She could feel it seeping into the ground, back to the element. Then, that last drop, the one she could always use to ask the elements to fill her up, that too was gone. Like a pin popping a bubble, that final connection to earth was severed.

She sensed the Dryad nearby. Could sense her mirth as Suleima grasped for the connection.

And then, it was gone.

She sat up quickly, in a panic. Gage shot to his feet, at her sudden move, alert and ready to fight. She grabbed for her pack and searched frantically for her supplies to recharge her magic. She forced herself to take a calming breath and started. Methodically, as calmly as she could, she performed her ritual. The green, northern orb sputtered and dissipated almost as soon as it had formed. She continued the ritual— she had used a lot of her water and air magic to release Gage. She continued to reach for the earth, but it was elusive.

Although she was tired, she repeated the ritual as soon as she ended the first one. But the earth orb dissipated again. "The sacrifice," she muttered. Her heart sank.

"What sacrifice?"

Suleima took a deep breath. "My power is my payment."

"Wait, what?"

"Damn," she hung her head. Already, her soul felt empty. The feeling—that she wasn't alone but surrounded by all living things—was gone. Even when she wanted nothing more than to hide away and heal, she had never been alone. The plants and animals that surrounded her cabin were always a presence in her mind, giving her a connection to life. It was all gone now. The birds were mere specks in her mind, not truly a presence, her only connection with them now through the air they glided on. The vibrance of the colors in the plants were dulled to her senses. The emptiness threatened to engulf her. Tears filled her eyes, but she blinked them away, and took a fortifying breath, "Nothing to do but continue. I do not want to stay around here any longer than I have to. Let's get moving. I'll need to rest earlier tonight."

"Please explain to me what you are talking about. Who are you talking about? What happened to your green orb?"

"While you were in the ground, I was trying to use my earth magic to free you, but it wasn't working. The earth was pushing back. It wasn't working like it should have. When I pushed the air bubble down to you, allowing you to breathe, I was pulled into a vision by the earth elemental. She was not at all pleased that I am here. She wanted me to leave you there. I refused. She asked me what I would sacrifice to continue. She refused to let you go when I wouldn't sacrifice you, so I found a way to release you myself. As payment, as my sacrifice, she has taken my power of the earth. It is my primary power." Suleima's voice softened. "As long as I can remember, I've always been able to feel the earth breathe, to feel nature and the animals surrounding it. It's so lonely. . . ."

"I'm sorry you were forced to make that sacrifice. Had I known . . ."

"There is no reason to be sorry, Gage. It wasn't a question whether or not to sacrifice you to continue on. It isn't an option. Never was. As I told the Dryad, you are not mine to sacrifice. I made a promise to Kaly; I would make sure you return home. I intend to keep that promise. Even if I hadn't, this is my journey, my fight, my spell." She stopped midstride and looked at Gage, "I'm about to ask a favor, and I would like you to consider what it could mean before answering."

"I'm not leaving you, Suleima. You don't need to ask. It will not happen. If I had not been here, would you have been the one buried? Would you have been able to free yourself? Consider me cannon fodder, whatever. But I am not leaving. I will trail behind if you try to leave me or sneak away. What kind of danger could I get into if we split up now?"

"You don't play fair."

"Apparently, neither do the elementals."

Chapter 8

They walked for a while before stopping for a quick bite to eat. The journey was quiet. Too quiet for Suleima. She was finding it unsettling, not being able to feel the earth as she always had. It was such an integral part of who she was, and who she had been for as long as she could remember. Everything was connected to the earth, but all of a sudden, she wasn't, and it terrified her. As she sat there eating, in the quiet, the fear threatened to overwhelm her.

Gage must have noticed her hand shake as she lifted a piece of fruit to her mouth. "Are you OK?" he asked.

"I feel like a piece of me is missing." Suleima paused for a moment before continuing, "I can't defeat Dirrin, even with the spell, without access to magic. Dynasira will need to find another shaman to perform the spell if we retrieve the Flame. Earth was my primary power. My strongest power."

"You won't be fighting alone. My wolves are with you. Dynasira is with you. We will help you to do whatever is necessary in order to defeat Dirrin."

"I will not be strong enough after this trip. We need a backup plan." It took effort, but Suleima was able to call a pigeon to her, pulling with air, rather than intertwining her earth and air abilities. She wrote a short note to Dynasira with an update and sent the pigeon to deliver it. "That will get Dyna thinking. The more of us that can work on this, the better. I'm running out of places to look for allies, and we are so outnumbered. It terrifies me to have to go against Dirrin again, especially at such a disadvantage. We are already so low on numbers, and now this . . ."

"We will find a way to make it work."

"I've been trying to remember the story as Erist told it to me so many years ago. He loved to tell stories, especially those about how he was taught to use magic. His mentor had been a strong shaman. To hear him describe it, Erist had never met a stronger practitioner. But, as I try my hardest to remember, there are no stories about his mentor after this trip they took together. Xavien's story ended up here on the mountain. Whether by death or loss of power, he was no longer a participant in Erist's life and training. I have to believe that the same fate will befall me."

"I won't let any harm come to you," Gage said.

"You don't have the ability to promise that, Gage. While I appreciate the sentiment, I must bear all consequences of my choice to take this journey."

"That doesn't mean I won't do everything I can to make sure you get off this mountain in one piece. You are more vulnerable now. Have you been trained to fight, without using spells?"

"Nothing specific. I've picked up a few things. Most of what I have picked up though has been fighting Dirrin's minions, and usually only after I've trapped them with my magic."

"We better change that." Gage put away the remnants of lunch and pulled Suleima to her feet. He pulled a knife from his boot, walked around a bit, and grabbed a thin, flexible branch from the ground. He tried bending it several different ways, and then used his knife to trim down each end. Then he cut a notch in the top and the bottom of the stick. He cut a length of the thin rope he'd brought in his pack, tying it on each end of the branch and pulling it taut.

Gage walked over to Suleima and looped the bow over her body, resting it on her shoulder. "Watch what sticks I collect as we make our way along the path. Straight sticks, which are dead and dried, are the best. Pick up any you find, and I will show you how to prepare them when we stop for the night."

By the time they stopped for the night, they had made it to the Northwest side of the mountain. This time, Gage spotted the out-cropping of rocks they could use as a shelter for the night. Suleima felt useless, unable to scan their surroundings for threats or areas of safety where they could bed down for the night. She had no ability to manipulate the earth to make their makeshift beds more comfortable for the night ahead.

Again, they strung their tents above the top of the rocks and cov-ered it with leaves. Suleima attempted her ritual again, but again, the green orb faltered and dissipated, leaving her still disconnected to her powers of earth. She needed a moment to herself, so she headed down to a small pond she felt nearby. Drawn to the water, her connection to it, a lifeline in a sea of melancholy. Tears fell freely as she neared the small creek of fresh water. The loneliness she felt was overwhelming, a gaping maw that threatened to swallow her whole.

Purifying the water took more effort and time, as she could only manipulate the water. The earth stubbornly refused to cooperate as she attempted to sift out sediment. When the task was completed, she splashed the cold water from the stream onto her face, attempting to wash away evidence of her tears, and then trudged back to the campsite. A huge part of herself was missing.

Suleima did not want Gage wandering off hunting, afraid of him getting caught in another trap, so they sat to eat some of the foodstuffs they carried with them. She tried to keep up small talk to distract herself from the silence and loneliness she felt without her connection to the earth. Its absence seemed more palpable to her as she sat watching the shadows grow longer and the reds and oranges appear in the sky. She could usually feel the animals starting to settle in, while others began stirring.

Gage seemed to know she needed a distraction and pulled out one of the sticks they had gathered. He started a small fire and showed her how to use the heat from the coals to help straighten the wood. Then he whittled down the one end to a point and carved a notch in the back of the arrow for the string of the bow. Lastly, he showed her how to use the coals again, this time to strengthen the point he had put on the arrow. "If we come across any feathers, we can gather those to make fletchings on the arrows to help with balance and trajectory, but I didn't see any to pick up today."

Gage picked up two more sticks and handed one to her, along with a smaller knife. "Don't cut off a finger, please."

The two worked in companionable silence for a while.

"What brought you to the Amber Mountains to form your pack?"

"I had been there once, on a hunting trip with my original pack. I couldn't have been more than seventeen. I just felt a connection with it. Such peace when I was there." Gage shifted in his seat as if uncomfortable. "When I left that pack, I was unsettled, scared, and uncertain. I wasn't sure if I had made the right decision by leaving.

I didn't know if I would be a good leader. I only knew I could not tolerate that kind of treatment."

"That alone shows you had what it took to be a good leader."

Gage smiled slightly, "When I brought Kaly here, we were it. Slowly, we met other wolves, and they joined us. Then a few more. Until now, when we are a pack sixty strong. Most live near the pack house, in houses and cabins scattered over several miles. And, as you have come to know, we hunt up through the woods, sometimes all the way up to where your cabin is. The pack has grown so much, and I am proud to say all of our wolves are treated with respect, no matter their dominance or gender."

"That is certainly something to be proud of."

They finished whittling the remaining sticks they had collected into arrows. Before long, Suleima began to nod off. Gage covered her with a small blanket and prepared to take watch.

Suleima slowly woke, noticing the sun was starting to rise already. She started to sit up, but Gage, curled up next to her, in wolf form, growled lightly at her movement. "Gage, you didn't wake me up! And what are you doing as a wolf?"

He stood and stretched before walking a short distance away. She could hear him changing, so she went about preparing some breakfast and cleaning up around the camp. She was stiff and sore from sleeping on the hard ground. Moving helped her muscles to loosen, but she really missed the comfort of the previous nights. She nearly had all of the tent down and put away by the time Gage returned.

"I would have helped with tearing down camp."

"Why did you not wake me up last night?" she asked.

"You were exhausted. You needed the rest." He sat down next to her. "Besides, as a wolf, I'm able to rest and my wolf keeps up his guard. I have better command of my senses as a wolf as well."

Suleima snacked a bit on some crackers and dried fruit for breakfast. "You need to eat, Gage."

"I ate already. Caught a rabbit who ventured close to camp just a few hours before dawn. I'm good, I promise."

They sat in companionable silence for a little while longer before finishing the camp cleanup and packing away the final bits that remained.

"We should take it slow today. We don't know what we will run into next. And, if we go slow, I can teach you to use the bow. You also should keep the small knife, to repair or to make new arrows, and as a backup weapon. I'll teach you to use them both."

They walked for a couple of hours, and then Gage set up a set of targets. He demonstrated a few times how to aim and shoot the arrows, before handing them to Suleima to try. She struggled to hit any of the stationary targets. She was tempted to use her power over air to set the arrows on course, but that would defeat the purpose of training to use it, so she focused on learning the technique. Gage worried the arrows they had made would not hold up under repeated use, so he stepped in to help. He stepped behind her, wrapped his arms around her, and helped her to steady the bow. He nocked the arrow and aimed. Suleima was conscious, every moment, of the warmth she felt, standing so close. She tried to hide the hitch in her breath as he placed his hands on her hips to adjust her stance.

The arrow she released still missed, but it was closer. "Try again." He nocked another arrow and adjusted her hold on the bow and her elbow on the arm that held the string. He whispered close to her ear, "Release the string and follow through." Her eyes closed for a moment. She took a steadying breath, and released the arrow. The arrow glanced off the target, but she'd hit it.

He handed her another arrow, this time, stepping back and allowing her to nock it. This time, it was a direct hit. She turned and faced him, her smile lighting up the otherwise cloudy afternoon.

"Repeat that." He handed her arrow after arrow, and she continued to hit the target most of the time.

"When we get off this mountain, I'm getting you a bow. You are a natural."

She smiled shyly. "The student is only as good as her teacher. Thank you. At least I won't be completely helpless without my power."

They picked up all of the arrows, as well as a few more sticks to make additional arrows, had a quick bite to eat, and headed off again. Suleima could sense they were closing in on a small body of water. She wasn't sure if she should be happy about the fresh water source, or terrified it could be another challenge. She paused a moment. She turned to look at the path behind her, and it shimmered. The mountain seemed to be pushing and pulling them to satisfy its own timeline. The day before was nothing but switchbacks that should have kept them from covering much ground. Now, they had to have covered much more distance than should have been physically possible, as they were approaching the west side of the mountain much faster than they should have.

"Gage, we will come upon water in the next hour or so. As soon as we reach the west side. I'm not sure if this is good or bad."

"We will take it head-on. I am here to help."

"Will you reconsider? I don't want you getting hurt."

"Yeah, no. Not going anywhere. We are in this together, like it or not."

Suleima took a deep, steadying breath and forced herself to put one foot in front of the other.

"Please shift."

Gage's surprised look told her it was the last thing he expected.

"I don't know what we will face, but you are faster and better able to defend yourself as a wolf. I can't have you hurt."

Gage took her hand and squeezed it lightly before walking a short distance into the woods behind some cover. Suleima sat in the grass alongside the trail, running her fingers through it, wishing she could feel nature as she always had. She tried burying her fingers in the dirt, but again, nothing. No connection at all. She picked up a fistful of dirt, sifting it through her fingers. The hum was gone. It no longer sang to her or called to her. She couldn't feel Gage changing into his wolf, couldn't sense any animals nearby, or if they posed a threat. She felt vulnerable, and she hated it.

Suleima was startled when Gage huffed a breath from where he had emerged on the trail to get her attention. She stood and gathered his pack, adding it to her load. Gage whined as she did.

"It is not heavy. And I should not have to carry it too long."

The two walked side by side up the trail, which was getting steeper by the foot. Suleima noticed the water called to her. As her secondary power, Suleima had always felt that connection, but even more so now, with the lack of connection to earth. Her step faltered for a moment, and Gage turned to look at her.

"I am pretty sure, when we round this bend, and the water comes into view, we will cross a boundary. I felt us cross one, just before you were sucked underground. Please, stay close, but stay behind me."

Gage's low growl indicated to her just what he thought of that plan.

"You may not like it, but I'm not about to let you get hurt. Suck it up, buttercup."

Gage bumped his hip into her knee, but he did fall back half a step. He may not like it, but he would listen; that was all she could ask.

Chapter 9

About a half hour later, Suleima finally came around the long bend and could see the lake ahead of her. She felt the barrier as they crossed and curled her fingers in the fur at Gage's neck. He had only stayed about a half-step behind, and if she could not get him to stay back, she would at least make sure he wasn't going to go anywhere.

She could hear singing, a lovely melody which drew her to the water. She continued to walk toward the lake, eyes darting from side to side, looking for anything out of the ordinary, hand flexing in Gage's fur to make sure he was still there. To reassure herself he was still unharmed. The music called to her, and she followed without hesitation.

She was knee-deep in the water when she felt Gage's teeth clamp down on her hand. She shook her head to clear it and looked at Gage, in the water right with her, but he still had a firm grip on her hand with his teeth. He growled low in his throat and backed up, pulling Suleima with him.

When they reached the shore, Suleima shook off his hold and removed their packs. "I hear music. It calls me. Promise me you will stay out of the water."

Gage growled and tried to go for her hand again. But he was too late. A large wave came upon shore, pushing Gage away and dragging Suleima in. With her last gasp of air, she screamed for him to stay away from the water and hoped beyond all hope he would listen.

Dragged near the center of the lake, Suleima's lungs burned for air. Using her powers, she tried to propel herself to the surface, but could no longer control the water. She pulled air from the water and formed it into a bubble, bringing it to her face and taking a gasping breath. She couldn't panic, could not react hastily. She tried to relax and allow the water to take her where it would, to take her to the challenge, so she could face it and move on.

She slowed, and finally came to a stop near the center of the lake. Only then did the water allow her to surface. A fog seemed to block the shoreline from view, and she hoped Gage was still there, safe from whatever was coming next.

A beautiful woman stood on a small island. Long, flowing blonde hair covered her bare chest. A ring of flowers made a halo on her head. A naiad. She stood on the shoreline, one leg slightly bent, like a vision of the birth of Venus.

"I am the protector of the water element. Why do you come here, child?" she asked. Her voice was musical and light, and it seemed to dance across the water to Suleima, who still floated at the surface.

"I am on a journey to find the Flame," she replied.

"You will never reach it. You bring with you an unnatural creature who must be destroyed." Her voice held a musical lilt that was beautiful, but not enough to veil the threat.

"He is no more unnatural than I. He comes with me to help save the world from true evil. The Flame is our only hope."

"Then you will fail!" she exclaimed. Her arms raised into the air.

Suleima felt a shift in the water and peered below her as best as she could. She could make out a large shadow below and went under to see what was there. A large snake swam at unnatural speed at her, its fangs extended. In a desperate attempt, she pulled at the earth below, trying to form a hand to grip the snake, but there was still no connection with her power over earth. Suleima grabbed the small blade Gage had given her.

When the snake was too close to react, Suleima used a burst of her power over air to propel herself just to the left of the snake, holding her right arm out with the knife in hand, slicing off a two-foot-long strip of the snake's flesh. It reared back. Suleima jammed the knife into the side of the snake's neck, just behind its head, but missed the spine. The snake darted for shore. With the knife still wedged behind its head, Suleima held on for dear life, yanking the knife free and rolling away only when they reached the shore.

Gage had been standing at the shoreline and snapped his jaws at the snake, drawing its attention, like a dummy. The giant snake darted for him, and Gage danced out of the way twice, before he was caught. Suleima dove for her pack and grabbed the bow and an arrow, steadied herself, and took aim, careful to aim for a part of the snake not wrapped directly around Gage. She missed with the first arrow but connected with the second in a meaty part, just below the head. Using her influence over fire, Suleima increased the temperature of the arrow, causing it to burst into flame, then added an extra push of air to increase the heat.

The giant snake let out a loud hiss and dropped a limp Gage to the ground, darting for the water. Suleima kept up the bursts of air until the fire was doused by the lake. She moved to stand between Gage and the snake, as well as the Naiad, who was now coming on shore.

"My snake must be fed." The Naiad spoke as if Gage was nothing more than an old slab of meat at a butcher's counter.

"Then feed it from any number of creatures in these woods. My friend is not food," Suleima retorted.

"You injured my snake. I must have payment." The Naiad's eyes grew dark and stern.

"You sent your snake after me. You sent your snake after my friend! I defended myself. I owe you nothing! I was not the aggressor!" Suleima was shouting. Her panic began to rise. Gage still hadn't gotten up and she needed to check on him, as soon as possible, but she dared not turn her back on the Naiad or snake. She allowed herself to take two steps back, until her heel bumped into Gage's ribs. She could feel the slow but shallow breaths he was managing but could also hear how labored it was.

"Payment!" The Naiad's hair blew forward as a wave hit the ground, conjured by her ire.

"I will not sacrifice him to you or anyone else! He came to help me on my journey. He has sacrificed the safety of his pack to accompany me."

"So be it." The Naiad and snake seemed to fade back into the lake and were gone.

Suleima dropped to her knees to check on Gage. He was breathing, but several ribs were likely broken. "Gage, you must wake up. You must shift. Please!"

After a few long moments, Gage stirred. His eyes were wild, searching the shoreline for danger as he struggled to get to his feet.

"It's safe. They are gone. Shift, Gage." Suleima said. A moment later, she could feel his own type of magic push and pull at him as his shift began. She backed away, to allow him to do so at his own pace. Close enough to protect him if needed, far enough to give him space and privacy.

The moment she stepped away, she felt an unpleasant and now-familiar pull at her own powers. Her access to her water magic was gone. After the first time, she figured it would be this way. By the time this was all said and done, she would be cut off from all of her magic.

She tried to block out the melancholy feelings that threatened to overtake her. To keep busy, she rummaged through Gage's pack to find him clothes. The packs, and everything in them, were soaked through from the wave that hit Gage. She pulled out a set of clothes for him and using her remaining powers over fire and air, she called the wind to her, warming and drying his clothes. She dropped the clothes where he would be able to reach them easily and backed away to give him space again. She dried her own clothes and sorted through the packs, drying what was needed and inventorying what could not be saved. More of their food stores were gone. They would need to hunt more, and she would need to dry as much as she could to preserve it for the remainder of their journey. The further up the mountain, the scarcer their wild food sources would become.

At that point, there was nothing left to do but wait, so she sat near their packs with her knife and worked at another stick, to replace the one she had used on the snake. When she finished with the arrow, Suleima performed her ritual to recharge her powers, and wasn't surprised not only the green orb, but now the blue orb to the west also immediately dissipated. It was longer than usual before Gage emerged, pulling his shirt down over angry purple bruises along his ribs.

Suleima stood, keeping her eyes downcast. "I'm so sorry you were hurt again."

Gage placed a hand under her chin and raised her eyes to meet his. "There is no reason to be sorry. You saved me. Yet again. I thought I was here to help you, not make it more difficult for you."

Suleima nodded solemnly. "Gage, will you consider—"

He interrupted. "I'm not leaving you to face this alone. Don't ask me to. We should get moving. I recall the giant snake coming at me, but not much more after. Maybe you can regale me with the tale, as we get away from this creepy lake." Gage was trying to lighten the mood, and while she did appreciate the effort, she had too much on her mind to even pretend to be lighthearted.

She could no longer feel the lake, or the many streams caused by the melting snow she had felt during this whole journey up the mountain so far. She was losing her connection to everything in nature. She needed to prepare herself to have no powers once this was completed. By now, she should have been used to loss. Erist, her childhood home, all of those who fought alongside her last time and died, even her own freedom, as she hid away to regroup and heal. Those losses would be with her forever, because of Dirrin.

Even so, each loss of her power over the elements was a new blow, a new injury to her soul, and she questioned how much more she could take before she broke.

She followed Gage around the lake, both of them giving it a wide berth, until they reached the other side of the trail and continued their climb. The vegetation was getting sparser, and they were only a couple days from the snow line. She could feel the air thinning and wondered how that would affect Gage's breathing, with his freshly broken ribs.

She must have inadvertently spoken out loud because he answered. "I will be fine. The air won't be thin enough to affect me until my ribs are completely healed. Shifting as quickly as I did helped to heal me faster. Also, as a Pack Alpha, I am able to pull from my pack to heal faster. Just as Kaly can pull from me, because of her connection to me, when some of the wolves get out of hand."

Chapter 10

Gage and Suleima walked in companionable silence for a couple of hours, staying on the trail unless one of them saw a stick they could use for an arrow. Suleima was very aware of the occasional labored breathing from Gage as the incline on the trail got steeper combined with the rib injury he sustained from the snake. She didn't dare clue him in that she was slowing down to help him; she knew that would be the last thing he wanted, so she deliberately exaggerated her own breathlessness to justify more breaks and the slower pace.

"Ready to tell me all about the snake?" Gage asked after a while.

"I hit it with an arrow on my second shot," Suleima said.

"Really? That's great!"

"I'm just glad it did not take a third. Could you work with me some more when we make camp tonight?" Suleima asked tentatively.

"Of course. Now, tell me the rest."

Suleima answered his questions but, otherwise, left the story to the barest of details. Only when he asked directly did she tell him she had lost her access to her water magic.

"Will this keep happening?" Gage asked, stopping her by placing a hand on her forearm.

"I can only assume so. Each of the elements are associated with a direction, north for earth, west for water, south for fire and east for air. We were on the north side of the mountain when we encountered the Dryad and the west with the Naiad. I have sensed something pushing us to each side of the mountain. I assume it will continue throughout the rest of the journey. Which would mean fire is next. Fire is my weakest element. Except in minimal activities, like starting a fire in my stove or campfire, I rarely use it. "

"I will help in any way I can, even if it means just staying out of the way, but—before you ask—no, I am not leaving you to face this alone. I have a part to play in this, and I won't abandon you to it alone." Gage paused a moment before continuing. "Do you not use fire because of your scars?"

"No," she said simply. "I have never had much of a talent in using fire. Erist always said it was because I am too kindhearted. But I don't know that is the case. Dirrin always had a heavy hand in fire and it always frightened me."

They walked for a few hours before stopping to make camp for the night. Gage and Suleima went about their routine, setting up camp and getting the fire started. Gage heard water nearby, and Suleima walked in the direction he indicated. She never sensed it. Try as she might, she was unable to purify the water as she collected it, so she filled all of the canteens she had available and hauled the water back to the campsite, where she was forced to boil it all to make it safe for drinking.

"We will have to carry more and more water with us. There will likely be less opportunity to collect it the higher up the mountain we go, at least until we hit the snow line." Suleima felt like she was failing.

How useful would she be by the time they reached the top of the mountain? Already, she was unable to sense danger from the wildlife around them and now she couldn't even help with the water.

The two of them sat near the fire and whittled more arrows in silence. It was too dark by the time they stopped to practice with the bow, so they planned to get up early in the morning and practice before leaving camp.

"While we are walking tomorrow, I'll work with you on hitting a moving target. Chances are, whatever you are aiming at won't just stand there to allow you to shoot it." Gage said.

"If only." Suleima yawned and stretched. "It will be slower going up the rest of the mountain. The path is getting steeper and narrower. It will also be getting colder. The air is already thinning."

"Rest again tonight," Gage said, then stood and started off into the tree line, "I will keep watch as my wolf. Maybe catch us some breakfast."

"Please stay close, Gage," Suleima said, "I don't want anything to happen to you, especially while I am low on abilities to pull from."

"Yes, Ma'am. I'll be back in a few minutes." Gage said.

Suleima laid down a little closer to the fire, because the chill in the air was much more noticeable. She was nearly asleep when she felt Gage lay at her back, keeping the chill at bay. She drifted off with a small smile on her face.

Early the next morning, as she emerged from the tent, Suleima felt an oddness in the air. She tried to pull at earth for more information.

Sighing, she quickly packed up while Gage shifted and prepared for the day's hike.

The early part of the hike was just like any other day, but Suleima continued to feel something approaching.

The sun was nearing its peak in the sky when it all became clear. "We need to find shelter," Suleima said urgently, "Now!" Gripping her pack tightly, she left the trail at a run, heading straight up the incline, hoping to spot an outcropping of rocks for them to use as shelter.

The wind whipped and howled through the trees, threatening to knock her off balance. She did her best to mitigate the wind, but the swirling snow it brought along with it blocked her vision and made the ground slick. Gage was keeping up with her, just barely. His breathing was labored. She grabbed his hand, both to help pull him along, and so she didn't lose him in the blinding flurries that had already left more than an inch on the ground. This storm wasn't natural, but they weren't on the east side of the mountain, so it couldn't be the air challenge yet, could it?

Her feet slipped beneath her, and Gage was the only reason she didn't land face first in the snow, but she heard the grunt of effort her sudden weight had caused him. "We need to get out of this, fast!"

"I thought I saw something before the snow hit." Gage had to shout over the roar of the wind, "About a hundred yards, that way." He pointed back toward the west side of the mountain.

Suleima switched directions and fought for every foot they traveled against the wind and snow. Her fingers were numb, the biting cold cutting through every layer she wore. She could feel the dampness seep into her clothes as the snow melted.

The roar of thunder stopped her in her tracks, and she looked toward the peak of the mountain. She gave a strong push of air, clearing the snow in front of her, so she could clearly see the reason for the roar.

She wasn't going to be fast enough. "Get down," she said, her voice eerily calm, "At my feet. Lie prone, and don't move."

Suleima dropped her pack and turned to face the oncoming threat. She tried reaching for water first, then desperately raked at earth, to no avail. She released the power she used to see the avalanche speeding toward them, but she could feel the rumble beneath her feet and sense the disturbance in the air as it barreled closer and closer. She took a deep, cleansing breath, closed her eyes, and visualized what she wanted to happen. She braced her feet, digging into the earth as best she could. She had never tried anything like this before and prayed that she had the strength.

With her next breath, Suleima sent out power in front of her, pushing away in both directions. As the speeding, dense wall of snow hit the front edge of her power, she screamed at the strength of the impact and redoubled her efforts. Her feet slid with the force of the avalanche, but Gage grabbed her legs, holding her in place. Her arms shook with the effort.

As the bulk of the snow roared past them, Suleima collapsed to her knees, careful not to land on Gage. Gasping, she put her hands on the ground in front of her, the biting cold of the snow now feeling good against her heated skin.

The wind and snow continued to swirl around them. "Are you hurt?" Suleima asked, gasping between each word.

"No. We should move. I think we are close. If we go this way, we should be at the escarpment. It looked like a crevice in the rock wall wide enough for us to fit through. That should keep us protected from the elements for a bit." He grabbed her hand and helped her to her feet.

Suleima's legs felt like overcooked noodles, but she trudged behind him, dragging her pack. A few minutes later, they reached the mouth of the crevice. The wind whistled as it whipped across the small opening, but it was deep enough to block out most of the wind and snow. Suleima started to shiver as the adrenaline from the avalanche wore off. Using air and fire, she dried them both, as well as their clothes. There was a tree just outside the mouth of the crevice, and Gage was able to rip some branches from it and break them up. Even though the wood was still green, Suleima was able to use fire to start a decent campfire to warm them, and she kept up a push of air to blow the smoke back out into the weather.

The snow blanketed the area. It was almost knee-deep in some areas already, but it seemed to be slowing. Gage stood at the opening, staring out into the storm. "This isn't natural, is it?"

"I don't think so. Storms can pop up unexpectedly on a mountain, but this . . . this is something else."

"That display of power out there—how did you direct the avalanche around us?"

Air isn't my strong suit, so I took the path of least resistance. Instead of trying to push the snow away from us, back to where it came, I created a wedge of air that pushed it to either side of us. Once I had it directed, I let it flow as it would. I am just glad it worked. I didn't think I'd be powerful enough to do anything." She stood and walked to her pack, pulling out supplies to recharge her powers. Her hands shook.

Gage approached from behind and laid a comforting hand over hers. "You are powerful enough. You need to practice believing in yourself. The rest of us already do." He stood, then, and headed to the mouth of the crevice, "The snow's letting up. I'll see if I can find us some dinner nearby. I won't go far."

Suleima stayed where she was for a moment, letting those words sink in. She knew that Dynasira and Gage believed in her. But . . . all those lives lost already. They had believed in her, and she had failed them.

She stood abruptly. She didn't have time to wallow. She needed to recharge and be prepared in case anything else popped up before the day was through. They'd stay here through the night. Hopefully, the extra rest would allow Gage to heal from his rib injury.

Chapter 11

The next morning, Gage was gone when Suleima awoke. She could hear him just outside the crevice, shifting. She started packing away her bedroll and bringing the fire back to life. As she sat back down, a pigeon landed next to her. Dynasira had sent a response. Suleima took the note from the bird's leg and sent it on its way.

She had just finished reading the note when Gage emerged from the tree line. Suleima looked up, wondering how much longer they would have trees to give them shelter and firewood.

Gage dropped a couple of rabbits next to the fire and prepared them to cook. "Hopefully, these will hit the spot. A nice warm breakfast on this chilly morning."

"Thank you for breakfast." She handed Gage the note, "Dyna sent a reply. There have been no attacks since we left. She is not sure if there is anywhere else to look for allies. She knows a few magic wielders, but she's not sure if any of them would be willing or able to perform the spell. She wants to wait until we return to speak with any of them."

"I agree with her there," Gage said. "We want as few people as possible knowing about this spell. But we need to get the flower before that is even an option. For now, let's cook up breakfast."

When they finished their breakfast, Gage set up a few stationary targets for Suleima to practice on. It was not long before she was hitting the targets consistently, so they packed up the rest of camp, gathered up the arrows, and headed out. Suleima kept her bow in her hand, with an arrow nocked, so she could shoot at any moving targets they found along the way. Maybe she could even shoot them some lunch or dinner for later. The snow only slowed them down for the first mile. Past that point, there was no snow to be found. It was cold, but they at least had solid ground to walk on.

It took many tries, but by the time they were ready to stop for the night, Suleima was hitting a moving target about a third of the time. She had even managed to shoot a large bird for their dinner. The meat was a bit tough, but it was warm once they cooked it over the fire they had lit to keep them warm in the cold evening. Suleima would need to add more layers of clothing the following day, as temperatures were rapidly dropping, and they were quickly approaching the snow line of the mountain.

"We will reach the fire challenge some time tomorrow, I'm sure. We are getting close to the south side of the mountain," she said as they settled in for the night.

"I will shift again tonight. Not only will I stay warmer with fur, I can see and hear much better in the dark. I feel like I have been more at ease keeping watch at night with those heightened senses, and you need to rest up for whatever the fire elemental has in store for you." Gage headed out to shift.

Suleima tucked her chin to her knees and wrapped her arms around her legs, trying her best to stay warm, and gazed into the fire.

When Gage returned and sat next to her, she spoke softly. "Please, stay back tomorrow. When we approach the challenge, I will let you know as soon as I feel the shift, the barrier we cross that starts the challenge. When it happens, I need you to stay outside of the barrier. I will not have you hurt again."

Gage growled in response.

"Yeah, I know. But if you are safe, then I don't have to worry about you. I can concentrate on the challenge without any distractions." Suleima placed her left hand in his fur. She wished she could feel the softness of it better, but the scarring on her hand prevented it. She said goodnight, went to her bedroll, and covered up, colder than the air should have allowed. Her mind spun with worry. She couldn't shake the feeling that tomorrow may be one of the worst of the challenges. Her lack of talent with fire was an obvious problem.

Her fear of fire was another.

The roar that woke her was deafening. Gage stood between her and the sound, his hair raised, and snarled right back. Looking up, she saw the enormous, white-furred creature standing on two legs in front of them. Suleima grabbed the bow and arrow and stood. She barely reached the creature's middle. Gage made a move to confront it, but Suleima grabbed a handful of fur at his nape, stopping him. With his pack by his side, Gage could take it down, she was sure, but on his own, at the very least, he would be hurt.

All that stood between them and the yeti was the remains of their campfire from the evening before. The yeti took a step forward. Suleima pushed air at the embers of the fire and pulled on fire, causing the flame to jump eight feet in the air. The yeti reared back and roared. Each time the yeti tried to go around the flames, Suleima pulled them to block its path.

Gage pulled from her grip and swung his head, making a huffing sound. She nodded at him, and he turned, running around the flames. He snapped at the yeti's leg and then bounced out of the way. Suleima shot the flames back up between Gage and the yeti as it advanced toward the wolf.

The yeti howled in pain as the flames nipped at its arm.

Gage again rounded the flames, bouncing in, snapping, and bounding back out, Suleima keeping the yeti separated from Gage by flames. This continued until Gage had the yeti facing away from her. Suleima dropped the flames in front of her and released an arrow. It sailed over the yeti as it bent to grab at Gage. She flared the flames between it and Gage again, firing a second arrow, catching the yeti in the meat of its shoulder.

The yeti rolled its head, yowling in pain. She dropped the flames to her left as Gage headed back to her from the right. The yeti tore out of the campsite as fast as it could, Gage trailing behind at safe distance.

Suleima dropped her bow, wiping the sweat from her face, caused by the heat from the flames and the effort it had taken to keep the flames going. She looked up to see the sun barely beginning to lighten the sky. She sighed. There would be no more sleep. Suleima picked up her bow and then began packing away the bedroll and getting out some of the remaining food for breakfast, awaiting Gage's return.

She felt the clouds approaching. The air told her there would be rain to accompany their trek that day.

Chapter 12

Gage emerged and dropped two rabbits at her feet before grabbing his pack in his jaws and heading to a secluded area to shift. While he shifted, Suleima stoked the fire again with a push of her magic, getting it warm enough to cook, and cleaned the rabbits.

"We made a pretty good team." Gage placed his pack on the ground not far from the fire.

"We did," she agreed, "I think we did very well, working together. I only hope that the rest of our ragtag band of warriors can learn to do the same as quickly."

"A common goal can unite so many different types of people. I believe that in the end, our side will prevail."

"I have to believe that as well," she replied quietly, "If not, then I have to face that I am leading yet another group of honorable people to their deaths, and I don't know that I can bear the weight of any more."

Gage approached her, placing his hand on her shoulder, "You may be leading us all now, but even if you weren't here, this fight would happen. We have a better chance *with* you."

"I can't even get us fresh water. I'm not going to be any help when Dirrin shows up with his army of evil," she began, "And that is assuming that I can complete the remaining challenges without dying."

After a bit, he spoke, "You will get through this one with flying colors, just as you have each of the other challenges."

"But can I get through this one without you being hurt or killed?" she asked.

"I am a grown man and a werewolf, Suleima," he said, as if she hadn't noticed. "I can take care of myself. It is not your job to protect me."

She disagreed. It was her responsibility to take care of him. He had come with her to help her. He would not be here without her. He wouldn't be in danger without her. If not for her, Dirrin likely wouldn't even be on his radar.

As soon as they finished eating, they packed up what little remained of their camp. Walking side by side, they talked of nature and what drew them each to the forests and woods. He enjoyed the trees and the wildlife, the ability to run free in his wolf form. The thrill and satisfaction of a successful hunt and the quality of a freshly caught meal were bonuses to his ability to hunt anytime he chose. The acres of land that he owned and the miles of forest beyond gave him, and his pack, plenty of space and privacy to hunt and run and howl any time of the month, not just around the full moon when the call to be a wolf was at its highest. He could run for miles in the woods and never meet another person. He also saw all of that same space as his territory. As such, it was his responsibility to keep that area and all that lived in or around it safe. He took that responsibility very seriously, and that was the reason he was here on this mountain. He would keep the people in his pack and the people who lived in the surrounding area safe from any dangers that he could, or he'd give his life trying.

The peacefulness of the wooded areas drew her, calming her, rejuvenating her. She even still felt the draw to be in the forest, even without the connection to her earth power, and she could not imagine being anywhere else. Living in the city, as she had always done before, she had never felt this kind of peace. She understood the view Gage took when it came to the woods. But the role he played and the way that he viewed the woods, although different than hers, was just as vital in the health of the forests, keeping the circle of life in balance. She foraged and found healing herbs and, in general, found the surroundings as whole to be healing. The quiet walks she took helped her to find her center and her balance and also allowed her to practice some of her skills with magic. Although currently missing, she could remember the keen and comforting sensation of knowing where each of the living creatures were that surrounded her in the woods, allowing her to get close enough to see them or to avoid them when necessary. The feel of a nearby stream, calling her to feel the energy of the water as it washed over her fingertips. The hollow feeling where those sensations used to be brought tears to her eyes, but she refused to let them fall.

The peacefulness of the surrounding mountain stuttered. Suleima felt the barrier and stuck her hand out, stopping Gage. "We are here. Please, stay right here. I'll come back for you. But please stay here."

"I don't like this, Suleima."

"I know. But I'm asking you to do this for me."

Gage took her right hand but nodded reluctantly. "Take care of yourself. If you're not back here in the next hour, I'm coming in after you."

She looked down at their joined hands, then up into his eyes, "Agreed. In *two* hours. I'm not sure how long it will be until I meet up with the elemental. Please stay back until then."

He nodded and then released her hand. "Good luck."

She curled the fingers of her right hand into a fist, resisting the urge to forget what she was making him stay back for. She felt safer with him, but she could, *she would* do it on her own. She straightened her shoulders and continued up the trail.

An unnaturally warm wind blew her hair back. She turned to look behind her and saw Gage, still standing just outside the barrier at the edge of the trees. She glimpsed a shadow behind him, and she was about to yell out a warning when the elemental appeared to her left. A phoenix. The large bird was bigger than the thunderbirds. Its feathers were bright red, orange and yellow. The tailfeathers alone were at least twenty feet long.

It let out a long, high-pitched squawk. "I am the Phoenix, protector of the fire element. Why are you here?"

Suleima sighed heavily. "I am here because I need the Flame. People are in danger, and the Flame is the only way to save them."

"You will fail. You are weak. You have no power over the fire."

"And you will just take what little power I have when this is all said and done. I am still going to get the Flame. I will not be frightened away."

"You may have successfully navigated the trials of earth and water, but they're right. You will not succeed while you travel with a spawn of Volos. You cannot escape the danger he puts you in. You must leave him. Send him away."

"I will not abandon him. I will not sacrifice him. I will not bow to your demands. That is not who I am. I will never be!"

"Fire is flame. Fire is passion. You will regret your choice in the end."

Suleima looked at Gage. Even from this distance, she could see his eyes widen with surprise. One minute he was Gage, the next, he was a wolf. There was no long transition. It was an instantaneous change, just like Dynasira. Then he charged. He ran at full speed, directly at her. She held her hand up in an attempt to get him to stay where he was, but Gage was not in those wolf eyes. She could see it, even from this distance.

He ran full out, and she could see the snarl on his face, hear the growl as he neared. And he was running straight at her, *for* her.

When he was in range, he lunged for her. She barely turned in time, felt the snapping of his jaws right next to her ear, where her neck had been just a moment before. His momentum carried him past her, his ribcage slamming into her shoulder and knocking her to the ground.

Suleima turned in time to see him turn from where he landed and head straight for her. He jumped on her this time, pinning her to the ground. His first bite caught the sleeve of her coat and ripped a piece free, that piece turning to ash in an instant. The sleeve of her coat smoldered before bursting into flame. The next bite caught her left hand. The searing pain felt just as it had when Dirrin had attacked her with fire. The scar tissue did nothing to lessen the burn. The fire on her sleeve spread. Suleima reached for the water element, intending to pull the moisture from the air to douse the flames. Nothing. She pulled at fire, trying to extinguish the flames. Again, she came up empty.

Suleima didn't want to hurt him. She refused to pull the knife, and the bow was currently pinned between her and the ground, so even if she wanted to use it, it was not an option. "Gage!" she screamed, but she wasn't surprised when it had no effect. "Forgive me." She said simply.

Suleima pulled on her power over air. She created a vacuum within an air bubble, blocking all air from within and surrounded herself and Gage with it. Using the only power she could, she smothered the fire that had begun to consume her coat and burn its way into her skin. It also pulled the air from Gage's lungs, and hers.

She quickly became lightheaded, but she pulled harder on her spell. Gage sank his teeth into her skin. The burning sensation had disappeared, but she did not know if it was because she could no longer feel it, or because the lack of air had smothered it.

Then Gage collapsed.

Barely conscious herself, Suleima released her magic and drew in a deep, gasping breath. The spots in her vision were starting to fade. There was no sign of the Phoenix. Gage was unconscious but breathing. Cradling her left hand to her body, she maneuvered out from underneath Gage and took off her pack.

Suleima dropped the glamor over her hand to survey the damage. Although it looked bad, it was nowhere near the damage Dirrin had inflicted. She brushed off the loose, charred pieces of fabric from her coat sleeve and what remained of her shirt underneath. The damage was minimal. She placed her right hand on the ground to steady herself, as the world still felt like it was spinning, and instantly, she felt the drain of her magic. Her connection to fire, what little she had, was gone.

She pulled some bandages out of the first aid kit she had brought along, cleaned her burns and puncture wounds with water from her canteen, and covered them as best she could, using just one hand.

Then she moved back over to Gage. She sat for a few minutes next to him, a hand resting on his ribs, reassuring herself he was still breathing.

One moment, Gage was peacefully lying down, the next he was on his feet, his eyes rolling wildly. "Shh, Gage. Calm down. It is OK." His gaze connected with hers and he calmed slightly. He closed his eyes, stiffened his entire body for a few moments. When his eyes opened again, she read panic. "Relax. You are back in control. It is OK."

Gage whined, closed his eyes again, and his body stiffened. This time, with her hand on his neck to help calm him, she could feel the pull on his own type of magic. The magic of the shift.

"You can't shift back?" she asked.

Gage whined again in response.

"I will find some way to help you. I promise." She meant each and every word. She wouldn't stop until she was able to figure out how to help him. "For now, let's walk for a bit. I don't want to stay here any longer."

Suleima winced as she accidentally used her left arm to balance herself as she stood. Gage backed up several steps, hung his head, and whined.

"I will be OK, Gage. You weren't in control. *You* did nothing wrong." At another whine, Suleima dropped to her knee in front of him and cradled his face between both of her hands as best as she could manage. "I will survive this trip, and so will you." She needed to find a way to distract him as he had distracted her from her thoughts many times over on this journey. The guilt seemed to roll off of him in palpable waves. "I need you to suck it up right now and get us out of here. When we are far enough away, you can go catch me some dinner. Got it?"

Gage nodded.

Chapter 13

THEY OFFICIALLY LEFT THE cover of the trees: nothing to block the wind or to shade from the sun if it ever came out. Just shrubs and grasses remained. There would be no more sticks to gather for arrows or for firewood.

As they continued to walk, Gage stayed next to Suleima, his hip occasionally hitting her right leg. The wind whipped her coat around, but the one time she tried to button up her coat, her hand protested. The sound of pain she inadvertently made caused Gage to whimper.

"Did you see the pile of ashes we walked through when we left the site of the challenge?" she asked absently. "The pile you walked through?" At his nod, she continued, "I think that was what was left of the Phoenix."

Gage sneezed in response.

"If that was a laugh . . . I'd have laughed harder had you peed on it."

He bumped into her leg again.

"I could have sworn I saw something in the woods behind you, just before the Phoenix appeared," she started. "I was about to warn you.

I could swear I saw the Dryad. . . ." She needed to piece together what that meant, but she was at a loss for the moment.

It was beginning to get dark, so Suleima looked for a place to set up camp for the night. She spotted a nice area and pointed it out to him before going off the trail and heading up to it. He bounded ahead and sniffed around the site before sitting down, she assumed to show his approval of the area.

"I will start getting whatever I can find to try to get a fire going. I will be back in a few minutes." Suleima walked a bit further from the campsite and gathered what dried bushes and grasses she could find. It was difficult to find anything that would be large enough to keep the fire going for long. Taking her bow with her turned out to be a good decision—she stumbled upon dinner and actually hit it with an arrow on her first shot. She was getting tired of rabbit, but it would fill their bellies.

When she was within earshot of camp, she could hear Gage struggling with something and quickened her pace. When she reached camp, he was in mid shift. It seemed to be taking much longer than normal and was more painful, based on the sounds he was making.

She sat just outside of camp and waited. She let her mind drift back to the fire challenge. How was it that the Phoenix was able to make Gage shift instantaneously? How was it able to keep him from being able to change back? She tried to remember back to when she was learning the basics of how each of the elements worked.

Erist described it as a flow with the magic of water and air; fire and earth magic he referred to as a spark. But how would that pertain to wolf magic? Racking her brain, she couldn't come up with any lessons about shifters and their magic, let alone wolves specifically. There had to be some connection; otherwise, how could the Phoenix have influenced Gage's change in any way?

Technically, a phoenix was a shifter, but only in the broadest sense of the word. The bird could renew itself by burning up into ash and remaking itself. As far as she knew, it wasn't able to shift into any other form of human or animal.

It was ten more minutes before his shift was complete. His movements were very stiff as he stood and got dressed. She stayed where she was until he was fully clothed. He sat near the bedrolls and dropped his head to his knees.

Suleima sat on his left. She could see beads of sweat still pouring down his face. "You OK?"

"Not really. I had no control. I would have never—"

"You have nothing to feel guilty for, Gage," she interrupted. "The elements are doing their best to test me and you. We can't let this become a problem for us. I am fine. You are back on two legs, and we have made it through three of the four challenges. Well, three of the four elements. Who knows what the hell awaits us after that? I can't imagine it will be a good time."

"Your arm. And hand," he said, then gestured to the bandage she had sloppily wrapped.

"I am fine. The burns are all superficial. The scarring from before mitigated some of the damage."

He reached for her hand, but she held it back. "I need to help you to wrap that up. It is not very secure. It needs to be tighter to keep out the dirt."

"How about we get the fire started and camp set up? Once the fire is going, I can heat some water to clean it, and then you can help me bandage it better." She stood and picked up the kindling she had gathered.

He reluctantly agreed. The two of them worked quickly. Suleima tried to get the fire started but failed to get more than some smoke.

She was only just now realizing that even though she didn't use fire much, the loss of it was still having an impact.

"I'll take over here for now. Give your hand a rest," Gage said, taking a handful of kindling from her and kneeling beside her.

"I don't know if I can do this, Gage. I'm becoming more of a burden. I can't sense dangerous creatures, get clean water. I can't even start a fire anymore!"

Gage took her unbandaged hand in his. "You can do this. You have gotten us through every challenge so far. You aren't a burden. The sacrifices that you make at every turn prove how much you deserve to get the Flame. We will succeed in this. You and I will reach the peak of this mountain. You have to believe that. I wouldn't have left my pack behind if I didn't believe that we would come back with the Flame in hand."

She wiped tears from her eyes and steeled herself. He was right. She needed to believe that they could do this despite the obstacles. If not, they were wasting their time. She needed to not only show that she was worthy through these challenges, but also *believe* in her worth, as she believed in their cause.

She left Gage to handle the fire while she set up the bedrolls. Together, they were able to quickly put up the tent, and then they sat to address Suleima's hand.

Suleima hadn't replaced the glamour on her hand since the injury, so the scarring was plainly visible. There were several new puncture wounds from Gage's teeth and a couple of new blisters raised. The skin was raw and bright red with areas of white scattered through. She was relieved to see the burns were minor. Her forearm was in nearly the same condition.

She took off her coat and allowed him to inspect and help clean her wounds. When the wounds were sufficiently cleaned, she handed him a vial, which she had brought with her, containing a salve she had made from herbs growing near her cabin. He carefully dressed her arm and hand with new, clean bandages, making sure they were tight enough to keep out dirt, but not too tight and cutting off the circulation. When he finished, he sat silently with her hand gently nestled between both of his.

"I had no control over my wolf. My wolf had no control. My wolf feels safe with you. It never would have attacked, even without me in control." He paused a moment before continuing, "And I could not shift back. When I finally did, it took nearly thirty minutes. It was more excruciating than my first shift. At one point, I thought I was going to be stuck halfway in between."

Suleima knew little of shifters. She couldn't remember a lesson from Erist that explained it either. Dyna . . . she was Dragon, no matter which form she took. There was no *split personality* as seemed to be the case with Gage when he spoke of him and his wolf as separate beings. She handed him some dinner. "I thought by keeping you outside of the barrier, it would keep you out of the path of these elementals. I am sorry it didn't work out that way. I never wanted you to be hurt."

"You were the one hurt!" he yelled.

"I will survive, Gage. I promise. The injuries are only skin deep. The salve you put on my arm and hand will make them so much better by morning."

They ate. "You should go and rest, Gage. I will take first watch tonight."

"But your injuries . . ." he started.

"We both had a long day, Gage. I have gotten several full nights of sleep because of your wolf. You need to rest tonight. I will wake you in a few hours, so I can rest a bit."

"I should shift again . . ." Gage started.

"No. You *and* your wolf need to rest tonight. I will be fine. Please. For my peace of mind, please rest tonight."

"Do not leave the tent. Stay inside to stay warm, and wake me in a few hours." His statement brooked no argument.

"That I can do," she replied and climbed in after him.

Suleima sat, listening to the sounds of the night. This was the first night since she had lost her first power that Gage had not shifted and taken the full night's watch. She listened to the sounds of him settling in, then as his breathing evened out, she did her best to listen to the sounds outside to determine if anything was out of the ordinary. She sat with her knife in her hand, the bow and arrows within reach.

Once she was sure he was asleep, Suleima held out her undamaged hand, palm up. She closed her eyes and gave a slight tug on the air element. Taking a deep breath, she tried to visualize what she wanted, a small glow in her hand, but when she opened her eyes, there was nothing. The lack of result did not surprise her in the least. It was hit or miss whether she could control fire enough to pull a small glow of light in her hand on a good day, with use of all of the elements. With fire gone, the pull of air was nothing more than a fan. Sighing, she let go of the air and pulled a small flashlight from her backpack, along with her books. Keeping the light dimmed so she did not disturb Gage, she delved into her books, looking for any basic information she could find on the elements first.

Her books referred to the elements the same way Erist had: a *spark* for fire and earth, a *flow* of air and water. She closed her eyes and tried to visualize how she had always used each of the elements when calling on them, focus on the feeling of the pull. A small smile appeared as she made the connection. She had not thought about the subtle difference in pulling each of the elements in many years. It was times like this she missed Erist. Earth and fire felt sharper, called with a quick snap of intention, whereas air and water glided into place with smoothness and gentleness.

Suleima continued to scour her books, looking for mentions of shifter magic, but came up empty. Refusing to quit, she sat quietly and tried to think through everything that she had seen and heard over the years about shifters. Dyna could shift instantly between one breath and the next. She was a water dragon, so Suleima imagined that water played some part in her shift. Agron, a dragon of the Clan Verana, had shifted in front of her many times. His shift was just as quick as Dyna's, but now that she was analyzing it, was it more abrupt? Less fluid? Agron was an earth/water dragon. She couldn't remember specifically taking notice when a Rojada dragon shifted. The fire dragons were elusive.

So, was some aspect of the magic used in Gage's shift based on fire? Is that how the Phoenix forced his change? Suleima had no idea if she was on the right track, but if she was, what could she do with that information? How could she use it to help Gage and his pack? She had a million questions but no answers. Yet. She was determined to find the connection.

It would be at least a day or two until they reached the fourth challenge. The rest of the journey would be slow going. She could feel the snow on the air. The trail they followed was already getting steeper since leaving the area where she met up with the Phoenix. The vegetation was getting sparser by the step. They left the larger trees behind days ago, and even smaller bushes were few and far between now. Tonight would likely be the last time they would be able to have a fire, as small and short-lived as it had been.

Despite the loss of her limited use of fire, the loneliness did not smother her as it had when she had first begun losing her access to the elements. Gage had something to do with that. She glanced back at his sleeping form.

It was dangerous for her to be distracted by anyone or anything right now, but in the dark of this night, she could admit to herself that she would not have wanted to be on this trial with anyone other than Gage. An Alpha wolf who was confident enough in himself to be able to step back and let her lead. Someone with the patience to work with her and teach her new skills so she could better protect herself, but also ready to fight for her, fight with her, and allow her to stand on her own to fight. She felt protected, but not smothered.

The events of today notwithstanding, he had been there for her each step of the way, as she had been there for him. They had formed an easy friendship, one borne of challenges and battles already fought, and those still ahead. Their journey, both up this mountain and beyond, was dangerous in the best of circumstances. She only hoped that they would both be standing and whole when this all came to an end.

As she turned to look at his sleeping form, she noticed his brow scrunched tightly. Then he began to thrash. She reached out with her unbandaged hand and he abruptly shot up into a crouch, a horrified scream piercing the silence of the night. His breathing was heavy. Sweat beaded on his face, his eyes darting around for danger.

"It's OK, Gage," Suleima said softly, "It's only a dream."

He looked directly at her then and closed his eyes. "But it wasn't just a dream. It happened. I lost control of everything. You were hurt." When he opened his eyes, they were haunted by the memory.

Suleima patted the bedroll he still crouched on, and Gage slowly sat down. "I still feel safe with you. I feel safe because of you." She held a hand up when he started to interrupt. "You told me earlier that I needed to believe in myself. You were right. I'm right when I tell you now, you need to *trust* yourself. We both know that your actions at the challenge were out of your control. You can't accept the blame and guilt for something that you had no control over."

Gage gave a wan smile. "Maybe you should be listening to your own advice. Erist's death, and those of the others in the battles against Dirrin, those deaths are not at your feet."

"Easier said than done, huh?" She smiled back. "Rest, Gage. It's not time for you to take watch yet."

When he laid back down, it took some time before his breathing evened out and she knew he slept. After a bit, she noticed his brow furrow again and lightly placed her hand on his hair, murmuring nonsense sounds in a calm and soothing tone until he rested peacefully yet again.

Chapter 14

Suleima and Gage switched off halfway through the night, him keeping watch so she could rest. When dawn broke, they ate a quick breakfast before packing up camp and heading out wearing nearly every layer they had brought. The wind was whipping and frigid. About an hour into their hike, they stopped seeing bushes as they followed the path. Grass was sparse, only appearing in small clumps near rocks here and there. She was right about last night's fire being the last. There would be nothing to gather once they stopped for the night to build one. The rocky path got slippery, and the air was getting very thin. They only made it about half of the distance they had made on previous days. More breaks and a slower pace decreased their distance by a lot.

As much as she just wanted to get to the air trial and get it over with, Suleima was grateful for the slower pace. Her arm, though feeling much better, was still sore, and knowing how guilty Gage felt for his part in her injury, he needed the break as well.

"Gage?" she asked, during one of the breaks they took at midday to eat. When he looked up at her, she continued, cautious and watching for any sign he was uncomfortable with the direction she was about to take. "Can I ask you about shifters like you? How you change? What the process is?"

He looked at her, an odd expression on his face, but shrugged. "Uh, sure. Where did this sudden interest in shifters come from?"

She looked down at her feet before answering, "I don't really remember Erist teaching me much about werewolves, or even shifters in general. I'm trying to figure out how the Phoenix was able to have so much influence over you and your wolf. I've never before had a friend who was a werewolf that I could ask." She could feel the heat rushing to her face, so she paused to take a drink from her canteen of water.

"The first shift usually occurs in late adolescence, though it can happen in early adolescence if the circumstances are right. It is usually triggered during a moment of tremendous anger or fear. It is typically a quick but excruciating process. Now, I can usually shift within ten minutes, or even push it to five if I can pull at the pack for help, though I try not to do that unless it's very important. It is painful, but nothing like that first shift. My first shift was around the age of sixteen. Naturals get to learn to drive cars; we learn to hunt and howl at the moon," he paused, a smile on his face. "All shifts are painful, but none so much as the first one. You don't know what to expect. You hear stories told by others, but you can't really know until you experience it yourself. You learn to relax into it, that the reward at the end of the pain is freedom and running with a pack that really gets you, and it makes the pain more bearable. But that first shift, that first bone to break and reform, all the coaching and promises of what is to come flees your mind and you are just in agony, unable to focus on anything else but the pain—like every muscle, tendon, and organ is on fire."

She started at his description. "Fire? What makes you describe it that way?"

"The body temperature rises during the shift. In human form, my temperature runs hotter, it is why I'm not as affected by the cold as another human would be, but as a wolf, my core body temperature is even higher. I don't quite know if the sudden rise in temperature is the cause of that sensation or if the shifting, breaking, and remaking of my physical structure is what does it. That first shift, it was like my whole body was on fire. As each bone broke and reformed, as the hair sprouted and the claws and teeth emerged, each part of my body felt as if I was sitting in the middle of a bonfire, but the fire was within as much as surrounding me. That first shift may only last three or four minutes, but it feels like hours with the pain."

"How did the shift feel when the Phoenix made you shift instantly? Was it more painful because it was so fast?"

He thought for a moment. "No. It was seamless. I don't remember even a flash of pain. One moment I was standing there and the next . . . I was charging you and unable to stop myself—"

Suleima quickly interrupted. "When you want to shift into wolf now, how does it start?" changing the trajectory of his thoughts.

He furrowed his brow in concentration. "I'm not sure how to describe it. I guess the best way is that I look for the spark. There is an inner spark that is my wolf. When I find it, I embrace it, almost wrapping it around myself, and he steps forward to take over."

Suleima's breath caught at his explanation. Is it really that simple, the connection with fire and the wolf? She would need to see if there was anything in her books at home that could help her see if she was right. "You have mentioned your wolf and yourself as separate beings. You in control versus your wolf being in control . . . or in the case of with the Phoenix, neither of you in control. Can you explain that to me?"

"I'm always in some form of control, or at least able to take it back quickly if I need to. I can leave my wolf in control, if I want to sleep for instance, and I can rest while the wolf keeps watch, but as soon as I wake, I am back in control.

"I feel safe with you, as does my wolf. If my wolf is uneasy around someone, I would never be able to fully relax when I am with that person either. I have never come across a situation where my wolf is at ease with someone I'm not, but it would seem my wolf would feel my unease, as I feel his.

"I use his instincts, even when I am in human form. As an Alpha, I have more control over my wolf than others. Each of us has some level of control, but the wolf can be slightly more or less dominant than the person. I remember everything that happens when I am shifted, even when I give control over to my wolf. There are those who only get bits and pieces if their wolf is in control. It is a balance that each person has to strike with their wolves. A young boy I knew refused to allow his wolf any control. He had not grown up within a pack structure and was taught to fear his wolf. Because he had so separated himself and his wolf in their spirit, when the wolf shifted, he would completely shut him out and he remembered nothing. Our spirits are divided but melded together. . . .

"I guess that makes no sense." He paused a moment before continuing, "A two-headed snake is the best I can come up with. Our bodies are one, but we have minds and instincts all our own. Usually, we learn to balance what each of us is good at, and no matter the form, we can follow the instincts of the one who is best equipped to deal with each individual situation. There are exceptions to every rule, and more control and cooperation happens with maturity. But in general, we all learn to live the best we can using both our wolf and human sides.

"In essence, we are two spirits within the same body, but we are so intertwined that we nearly function as one. If one half would die, the other half would follow. We are separate but dependent on one another." He paused again. "When the Phoenix was controlling me, controlling my wolf, I've never felt that kind of terror before. If you had not shifted position, I'd have torn your throat out the first time I lunged . . ."

Suleima stopped him with a gentle hand on his arm as the pain drifted into his expression. "That didn't happen. Don't feel guilty about things that never occurred. There are enough things that we all feel guilty about without having to borrow more." She stood and cleaned up what little they had left of lunch. "Let's get moving. We still have a long way to go today."

As they continued up the trail, Suleima filed away all the details Gage had given her during their conversation. The spark and sensation of heat had to tie in to fire somehow, didn't they? That had to be why the Phoenix was able to influence Gage's change. Could she manipulate that in some way to help him shift faster, less painfully? What else could she learn from the way he was changed?

She was excited about the possibilities, the help that she could provide to Gage and his pack, but nearly stumbled as the realization hit her like a physical blow. It wouldn't be *her* helping Gage and the pack. She could provide her insights to another shaman, but they would be the ones to wield the magic.

Chapter 15

THE NEXT MORNING, THEY were both stiff climbing out of the tent. Their body heat and layers of clothes helped to stave off some of the cold, but the hard, rocky ground was not a pleasant bed. They quickly packed up camp and headed back up the trail.

"We will reach the air elemental today," Suleima said. "The earlier the better. I just want this over with."

"Do you have any idea what you are going to do for this challenge?" he asked.

"Not a clue. The elemental will likely not be corporeal. Arrows will sail right through it, if they don't get blown off course first. The knife will be useless. I have no access to my other elements—fire could burn through it, water could drown it, earth could trap it—I have no idea what I will do. I am open to suggestions." She paused a moment. "I'm starting to figure out just how much about my magic I don't know. I still had many years learning from Erist ahead of me when Dirrin killed him. I thought that I knew a lot. I thought I was ready to do this on my own. This trial, if nothing else, has taught me that I still have so much to learn."

After a few steps, he spoke again, "If it forces my change, takes over my wolf again . . ."

"Without you here, I would have never made it this far. I would have never learned to make a bow and arrow or to shoot it. I would have never learned to use the knife to whittle. Those skills you taught me got us past that huge snake and the water elemental. Without my use of earth and water, I was able to see that, although I prefer to not use it often, I am capable of using fire, more capable than I believed. I'd never have tried to make a wall of flames against that yeti if I'd had access to my other powers." She walked a few minutes more before speaking again. "And you haven't shifted since the encounter with the Phoenix. Who knows, maybe those fiery fangs of yours are a gift you can use. If so, maybe you can bite Dirrin on the ass."

The two of them laughed. It was the first real laugh she could remember having in a long time. It was the first real laugh she ever heard from Gage.

And suddenly the urge to laugh was sucked away.

Suleima never felt the barrier this time. A sylph dropped in front of her. The shape of a woman in a long flowing dress with long dark hair floated, her wings beating slowly. She was right there in front of them, but Suleima could see the trail behind her, through her. No corporeal body to be had.

Gage made a move to step in front of her, to protect her, but Suleima blocked him with her left arm.

"I am the Sylph, protector of the air element. Why are you here?" Her voice, a whisper on the wind, like wind chimes far in the distance.

"I am here for the Flame. It is needed to defeat an evil force that threatens the balance of the world." Suleima was tired of the song and dance, but she was prepared for it.

"You proved you are able to wield your power over air. You even almost impressed me with your ability to save yourself from the avalanche I sent. But you speak of evil, and yet you travel with a child of Volos." Her creepy ghostlike arms raised in Gage's direction.

"I fail to see the evil in him. He is the Alpha of his pack. He does what he must to protect them. He protects me on my journey—" she started.

The Sylph interrupted, "Protects you on your journey? Are those new scars on your hand and arm not from him?"

"The injuries were no fault of his or his wolf. I do not blame him, nor will I allow anyone else to lay the blame at his feet. The blame belongs to the Phoenix. Just as his injuries were the fault of the Naiad's snake.

"I have seen true evil, and this man is not it. Evil is not in *what* someone is. Evil is in their actions. He has been in danger more than I during this journey. The attacks from the Dryad and the Naiad were directed at *him*, not at me. He could have left at any time. I *asked* him to leave! He has chosen to face dangers that were never meant for him, to help me, someone he only just met a few short weeks ago. He has chosen to stand against a truly evil person, who will kill without mercy and without hesitation, to save not only himself and his pack but the community as a whole. He will come with me to the end of this journey. I will not leave him behind."

One instant, Gage was standing just behind her. The next, he had been pulled into the air by a cyclone dropped from the sky. As he whirled around, she was able to catch hold of one of his hands. The pull on her arm made her injuries scream. The flesh burned, and the puncture wounds ached, but she refused to let go. She pulled, leaning back far enough to grab onto the edge of a large rock with her other hand to keep from being pulled into the cyclone herself.

She knew it was futile, but she pulled at her air magic, hoping beyond hope she would be able to use it, but the air no longer answered to her call. She would lose what remained of her power, if they made it out of this at all.

"Let me go, Suleima!" Gage yelled.

"Like hell I will!" She tightened the grip she had on him as best as she could. The past damage to her hand and arm left it weaker than her right arm, but there was no way she would be able to switch her hold. She let out a guttural scream of frustration. Even as her strength waned, she refused to give in. She would succeed. She had to. There was no other choice. So many people were depending on her to be able to get this Flame. It was the only way to defeat Dirrin, and even though she could no longer perform the spell herself, she had to get it so *someone* could use it to save the world as they knew it.

She reached again for her magic and felt it gone, but for a glimmer. She reached for that glimmer, her eyes locking with Gage's.

There was a moment of stillness, a blast of blinding light, and then the cyclone was gone, and so was the Sylph.

Suleima sat down hard, cradling her left arm in her lap. She felt it as the air magic was drained from her, but she was ambivalent to it.

Gage dropped hard to the ground in front of her with a grunt and stayed there for a moment before speaking. "What the hell was that?"

She just shrugged.

"Your eyes. I have seen you work your magic before. Your eyes turn purple. Your eyes were white! I mean, ALL white!" he said, stunned.

"Wait, what?" she asked, incredulously.

"White, your eyes were pure white!" he repeated.

"Aether?"

"Come again?" Gage asked.

"Aether or spirit magic," she replied. "I have read very little about it, as very little is known. It is supposed to be pure energy with unlimited potential. It is the source of all that is living, but to tap into that . . . ? I didn't think it was possible."

Gage stood up and reached for her hand. "Let's get out of here before that sylph thing comes back."

Suleima nodded, took his hand to stand, picked up her pack, and swung it on her back. She could feel the aether, now that everything else was gone, but she could not access it when she reached for it again. She did not know what it meant, but she was not going to wait here to try and figure it out. It was a puzzle for another day, and she still had to reach the cave to get the Flame.

Chapter 16

DUE TO THE THINNESS of the air and steepness of the trail, they did not talk much as they hiked until they stopped for the night. The trail was only wide enough for one person at a time now, and even then, there were times they had to hang on for dear life as they traversed an especially difficult area. The howling wind made it difficult to talk, even when they were side by side, so it left Suleima's mind free to analyze the conclusions she had come to over the past few days and to speculate more on the things that she felt she was so close to connecting. Could the connection between fire and Gage's wolf be so close that even she could figure out a way to manipulate it and help him in the long run? Fire and the wolf seemed to be completely unrelated at the surface. Where, how, and why were they connected? She knew the key to those last questions would lie in the origin story of the werewolves, and she continued to come up empty as she racked her brain trying to remember any lessons from Erist on shifter history.

They found a small area to camp for the night, just big enough for the tent, when the sky began to darken. Attempting the rest of the climb in the dark would be dangerous. Luckily, the mountain blocked most of the wind from the tent, so they were able to talk with one another without having to shout over the wind.

"So, I can't imagine we will just be able to walk into this cave, pick up a flower and leave," Gage said, taking a bite of jerky.

"I believe it will be another challenge of some sort," she answered. "When Erist told me stories of this mountain, he described the challenges as being unique to each person. He only said each of the elements would test the shaman who dared traverse the mountain. The flower is inside a cave, not far from the top, but the cave can only be seen once you have reached the peak. What awaits us inside . . . Well, that is a complete mystery."

"What can you tell me about this aether magic?" he asked.

"Not much more than I have already. I never knew it could be used at all. I just knew it was the magic of life. It is the spirit of all things—of space, of light, of dark. It is everywhere."

"Will you be able to use it again?" Gage asked.

"That's the million-dollar question, isn't it? I don't have any idea. I don't know how I used it the first time." Suleima paused before speaking again. "We are looking for a flower called The Flame of the Truest Heart. My best guess is that this test will be of my heart, my spirit. So I would assume that even if I could figure out how to access that power again, it would be useless."

"How is your arm?" he asked.

"Sore, but it is OK." Suleima pulled off the dressing on her hand. "I should probably reapply the salve and rewrap this. How are your ribs?"

"Good as new," he replied. Gage helped her to redress the injuries to her arm and hand, taking care to not cause more pain. "Do you think we will reach the peak tomorrow?"

"I can't imagine it is a lot farther. Travel tomorrow will probably be slow going. There may even be some climbing involved," she said, then yawned.

"Get some sleep," Gage said.

"Is there a first werewolf shifter story?" Suleima asked, yawning between words.

He was quiet for a moment. "It's been a long time since I've heard it, but yes, there is a story. Thousands of years ago, a young man grew angry with his family. He ran away from them to begin a life by his own rules. He wandered the world, his explosive temper getting him cast out of many villages. He became lonely and created a family. His wife, a human, grew worried about his temper and ran away, but not before she fell pregnant with his child. She went into hiding in the woods. The man found her, and once again, his temper bubbled over. But a pack of wolves stood between them to protect and defend her. The wolves brought her to the safety of a woman of the forest, asking for help hiding the wife. The woman of the forest blessed the wife and her unborn child, promising to hide them from the husband. As another measure of protection, she sent the wolf pack along to keep watch until the babe was old enough to protect itself.

"The woman had a son but was stunned to find a wolf cub in his crib one morning. She rushed back to the woman of the forest, demanding answers. 'I blessed your child with the ability to protect himself,' she told the wife. She laid a hand on the child's head and he became a boy once again. 'He will not change again until he must. But, when he does, he will walk the path of a man and wolf from that day on.'

"The boy grew up, running with the pack of wolves who stayed by his side and became his best friends. One day, after returning from a run in the woods with his wolves, the boy discovered that his father had found them. His childhood home was ashes; his mother had been inside. Crushed by grief and driven mad by anger, the boy shifted to a wolf. His mournful howl echoed through the trees for miles. He tracked his father through the woods, his pack at his heels ready to fight at his side."

When Gage didn't continue, Suleima asked, "What happened next?"

Gage shrugged. "That's all I've ever known. It's how we came to be and why we run with a pack." He paused a moment, then said, "It does seem to just end, but I've never known anyone who knows the story beyond that point."

"I hope I'm not being intrusive," she said quietly. "I just have so many questions about werewolves and why their shifting is different from dragons."

"I understand your curiosity. And if you ever find the answers, I'd be grateful if you shared the information." Gage absently fingered the frayed edge of a blanket that showed the scars from the bear attack early in their journey. "If we find out why we shift differently, could there be a way to change how we shift? Make it painless or in an instant? Then maybe I could better protect those around me."

"I hope I can help you with that. Do you have to wait a certain period of time between changes? Or can you change at will?"

"The more dominant the wolf, the more often you are able to change, but it takes a toll. It is draining after a time, just like when you use your magic. As Alpha, I can borrow speed and energy from my pack, if I must, but I rarely do unless there is an emergency. Even so, the change is still not instant.

"Sleep now. We will have a tough climb tomorrow, and who knows what else. You need to rest."

"Will you sleep as well? There is no good way to sneak up on us here," she asked.

"I would only do that as a wolf. And I'm not sure I am ready to test the theory about the fire bite yet. And if I couldn't shift back . . ." Shadows of guilt passed over his eyes.

"Shift, Gage. You need rest too," she said, resting her right hand on his forearm.

"But last time . . ." he started.

"That was not you. It was not your wolf," she insisted. "Shift. I trust you."

Suleima made herself as small as she could to give him as much of the tent as possible. This shift seemed to take the same amount of time as it usually did, and not the thirty minutes it took him the last time when he shifted back. Suleima gave him a few more minutes to acclimate himself before moving a muscle.

The moment she moved, Gage's wolf turned to look at her, and he wagged his tail like a dog.

"See, nothing to worry about."

Gage let out a long huff and then laid between her and the entrance of the tent.

Suleima was exhausted, but she wasn't sure she would be able to sleep. What would happen tomorrow or the next day? How would she be tested? Would she succeed? If she succeeded, who would she get to complete the spell? Would they be able to defeat Dirrin? The questions spun in her mind in a constant anxious whirl. She threaded her fingers through the warm, soft fur on Gage's side and took a deep breath. He had the sweet smell of a fresh run in the woods and the warm, musky scent that was all his own. Closing her eyes and focusing on those sensations, she was able to finally drift off to sleep.

Chapter 17

Despite their extra layers, they had to brace themselves against the cold when they emerged from the tent the next morning and packed up camp. Gage seemed in much better spirits when he shifted back with no complications and no residual effects from the fire challenge. Suleima took comfort in his calmness, but her mind continued to spin with all of the unanswered questions of what she would now face and whether she would succeed. Gage, seeming to sense her need for silence, kept conversation to a minimum as they packed up camp and headed further up the mountain.

By lunchtime, they had reached a point where ropes were needed to get the rest of the way up to the peak. They would reach the peak of the mountain just before dark, so they'd need to make camp one more time before they reached the cave. The climb was grueling, and the muscles in her arm and hand were screaming by the time they reached the top. Gage helped to set up the tent, ate some dinner, shifted; and they settled into their comfortable routine.

The following morning, just after dawn, Suleima emerged from the tent. Looking down the north side of the mountain, the opposite way from where they had climbed up, Suleima could see the mouth of the cave. Their destination. They would need to use the ropes and rappel down.

This was it. They would complete this final challenge, she would get the flower, and they would begin the long trek down. She was looking forward to finally going downhill, assuming she survived this next challenge.

She was determined to make sure Gage got home to his pack, to help Dynasira and the others, no matter what it cost her. She'd dragged them into this mess, she'd be damned if she allowed it to destroy their pack. Was she ready to give up and die? No. But she was not willing to sacrifice someone else to accomplish her mission.

Packs secured and ropes set, Suleima and Gage each pushed off and rappelled down the north face of the mountain. Within a few minutes, they touched down, just outside of the cave.

"There is a spell on this cave. It shimmers. I can't tell what kind of spell it is. Best guess, with the way the rest of this mountain has been, it will trigger the final challenge," Suleima said. "I will lead the way in. Stay close. Who knows what is waiting for us in there." Even standing there, the cave was difficult to focus on.

Suleima nocked an arrow onto her bow. Gage placed a hand on her back, alerting her to the fact he was back there, and the disappearance of his hand would indicate a problem behind her.

Steps inside the mouth of the cave, she saw it.

It was not a flower.

It was a red crystal, floating in the center of the cave. It seemed to glow, lighting the interior of the cave, so everything was bathed in a reddish glow. They took in their surroundings. They did not see anything besides the crystal, but it could not be that easy. It would not be that easy.

One minute, Gage's hand was a comforting anchor on her back, the next, it was gone. Suleima whipped around and nearly fell backward. Gage was caught in the claw of the largest dragon she had ever seen. It seemed to stretch the mouth of the cave with its body. It was a snowy blue color, its scales seeming to shimmer even in the minimal light in the cave.

"Drop him! It is me who is here for the crystal." Suleima shouted, stepping forward, aiming her bow.

The dragon responded by grabbing Gage's legs with his other claw. He pulled Gage in different directions. Gage screamed in pain.

Suleima screamed, dropping her bow, holding her hands up in surrender.

The dragon loosened his grip, no longer pulling on Gage. "You have come for the crystal," it spoke, its voice harsh and deep. "A sacrifice is required. There is no crystal without sacrifice."

"I will not sacrifice him! What is it with all of you? He is not mine to sacrifice. Even if he was, it is not an option!" Suleima shouted. "I will not sacrifice Gage. Pick a new damn topic!"

"You will not sacrifice him? This creature who is evil in nature. This creature who attacked you, bit you, caused burns on your already seared flesh."

"Gage did not attack me. That was the fault of the Phoenix, the fault of the challenges, not of him." Suleima stood firm, her back rigid, her feet planted. She was not about to give up.

"He has been repeatedly trapped. Forcing you to use your magic. Forcing you to lose your magic as you climbed the mountain. Without him, you would have arrived here with each of your powers intact," it said matter-of-factly.

"The hell I would have," Suleima argued.

"You were warned by each of the elements you would not succeed with him at your side. You did not heed their warnings. You were foolish. Now, you have nothing," he taunted.

"So they would have just let me walk up this mountain without any interference if I had not brought Gage along?" she asked.

"They would."

"Lies!" Suleima yelled. "Those challenges would have happened regardless. The stories are not myth! I am a student of Erist's. He completed this journey many moons ago. Time and again, I was told this story. Erist did not lie."

"Erist?" The dragon seemed to think about that for a moment, then continued. "A sacrifice must be made." Its grip once again tightened on Gage.

"Then take me."

"No!" Gage shouted. "You can't! Let me do this."

"I have one condition if I am to sacrifice myself," Suleima continued, ignoring Gage completely.

"You ask for special treatment?"

"No. There is a great evil threatening the world. The Flame of the Truest Heart is the key to balancing the scales. Many lives are at stake. I will sacrifice myself if you allow Gage to take the crystal. He needs to take it and the spell that is in my pack to Clan Azula. They can help him to find a shaman able to perform the spell." Suleima pulled Erist's spell book from her pack. "I will not sacrifice myself unless I know Gage can take the crystal and spell to someone else who can help to save the lives of all of those in the path of destruction headed their way."

"Sacrificing you puts all those lives in danger. You would risk that to save this creature?"

"He would do everything in his power to save the same people I am here to save. He would not be here otherwise. He would have turned tail and run after the encounter with the Dryad. You heard him; he was willing to sacrifice himself. I refuse." She stood firm. "That is the only option you have. Take me, and leave the crystal and spell book with him. Allow him to leave this mountain with both. He will do what is right with them. They are of no use to him otherwise."

Suleima grew tired and stepped toward the dragon. She stopped within reach. "I said to drop him! He is not your sacrifice! I am!" Suleima pulled the small knife she held, ready to attack with it if necessary.

The dragon looked down at her as if she was an amusing insect. It slowly lowered Gage to the ground, setting him on his feet.

Gage ran over. "You can't sacrifice yourself. They need you to perform the spell. They need you to save them. I can't do that. I will not let you do this."

"It is not your choice, Gage. It is mine. My choice as to what will be sacrificed. I have no power left. I am no use to the battle. At least you would be able to lead and defend your pack. I would be useless. I could not perform the spell without my magic. All you need to do is to take the crystal and the spell book to Dyna. She can find a shaman to perform the spell. I can't stress enough the importance of this spell. It is the only way to defeat Dirrin at this point. His numbers are too great, and so is his power. This spell will take away any of the power he has gained by killing others. Without that, he will be vulnerable. The shaman needs to use the recharging spell in the book to help translate the spell to take away the stolen powers."

"Suleima . . ." Gage was at a loss for words.

"It is OK, Gage. I never should have made it out of the first fight with Dirrin. I just need you to promise me you and Dyna will do this."

Suleima said, placing a hand to his face, feeling the roughness of the beard that had grown during their journey. "I can't thank you enough for all you have done to help me on my journey here. Take care of yourself." She planted a soft kiss on his cheek and stepped toward the Crystal Dragon.

Gage grabbed her hand to stop her, but she simply turned, smiled at him, pulled her fingers from his, and continued to walk forward.

The dragon's tail whipped behind her, effectively separating her from Gage. "He gets the crystal first." Suleima said, her tone indicating she would not back down.

Gage approached the crystal with caution, gently closing his hand over it. The power inside sang to her. Suleima nodded at her pack, which he lifted and placed on his back, after tucking the crystal inside.

"I can't leave you here," Gage said sadly.

"You don't have a choice," Suleima replied. "I am not a member of your pack. You have no responsibility to me. Please do as I ask, Alpha. Make my sacrifice one that counts." She gave him a wan smile and raised her hand in goodbye.

Gage hung his head and took a step toward the cave mouth.

Chapter 18

Suleima couldn't find the words, could not comprehend what she was seeing. Standing in front of her was Erist. She reached out, and her hand passed through him. A vision of him, but it seemed so real.

"Your sacrifice is noble, but you are still needed here. The crystal is granted to you. You have proven your heart to be pure, your intentions noble, and your actions beyond compare. Given the choice to sacrifice this man to save yourself or your powers, it was never a whisper in your mind. Despite your distinct disadvantage, you found a way, even learning new tricks from your companion to face the challenges on your journey. Never once did you consider using any dark magic to survive. And aether allowed you to pull from the magic within because of the goodness and determination in you. You make me proud, Suleima. I knew you could find my book. A slight nudge from me, the flicker of an idea in your mind, and I had faith that you could find the spell you need. I knew, with a small push from me and the wind, you could solve the riddle of the spell. I knew you had listened and would remember my stories of the great mountain. As I have foreseen, you have completed each of the challenges. I knew it would be you to face Dirrin, you who could defeat him. Only you would sacrifice everything for everyone else."

"He is so strong, Erist."

"He is strong. But you are strong. You are pure of heart. You are everything that is needed to defeat him. You have always had the strength. With the crystal and the spell, you now have the tools as well." Erist's image fluttered into and out of view as he spoke.

"But my powers are gone. How can I perform the spell?" she asked.

"Are they?" Erist gave her that goofy smirk of his.

She missed that smirk.

Erist held out a hand. She reached for it, and to her surprise, she felt his hand. "Your power never left you. It was always there, waiting for you. It will never abandon you. You only thought it was gone. Close your eyes, child, and you will find it."

Suleima did as she was asked. She searched and felt small glimmers tucked away. She reached for them and suddenly felt flooded with senses and power. She could feel the pulse of the earth again. She could feel the water, the air. Even her connection to fire seemed greater, though still less than the rest. She couldn't help the smile spreading across her face.

"Your wolf"—Erist gestured to Gage, who had taken a few steps and closed the gap between them—"has proven his worthiness as well. To survive as he has, to trust in you as he has . . . I approve." He said, winking at her.

Suleima was shocked but smiled, shaking her head at Erist. "Meddling old man. Besides, I must defeat Dirrin. I must survive that battle first."

"You will, child. You will have help. But, in the end, it will be you." Erist said.

"I will be forced to kill him, won't I?" she asked.

"Yes, child. He is beyond saving. You know that already. You will be fair, just, and quick. He is no longer the boy who you knew as a brother. He hasn't been that boy for many years now. There is nothing left of the young man you knew. Only death can bring him peace now. Be safe, Suleima. Be well. Be happy. You deserve all that and more." In a shimmer of the air, he was gone.

Suleima fell to her knees. Gage landed beside her a moment later.

"Are you OK?" he asked.

"Erist . . ." she started.

"I heard your side of that conversation, so I got that far. What happened?" he asked.

Suleima laid her hand on the ground, looking Gage in the eye. Her eyes, she knew, were bright violet. The smile on her face was so wide, she felt as if she could light up the cave.

Then she looked around, surprised herself. "Where is the dragon?"

Gage spun around. "I don't know. I felt like I was in a trance when the vision of your mentor appeared. It must have slipped out or disappeared. Or—" Gage stopped and walked a few feet, lifting a crystal scale. "Well, we didn't imagine him. That was sure as hell a crystal dragon. I thought Dynasira said they were a myth."

"She did. It is the protector of the Flame. Maybe since we earned it, it is done with us?" she replied. "As for Dynasira, she would have told me if she had known they were more than a myth."

"Well, we can show her this," he said, holding up the scale. Gage secured the scale in his pack of supplies and then headed to the mouth of the cave.

Suleima followed suit. "It looks like a trail about a hundred feet down. We will have to rappel again, then hopefully, we can hike the rest of the way."

They rappelled down to the trail and continued for a few more hours until it was nearing dark. Suleima found a good place to camp for the night and set up the tent. There were a few very small bushes, but she managed to get a small fire going to help warm themselves up.

Suleima took great pride in her ability to get the fire started quickly. She was able to call to the water in the earth, pull up a spring, and fill their canteens with fresh, clean water. She could feel the pulse of the earth again, sense the creatures that lived here on the mountain. She reached out her senses, looking for the Crystal Dragon, but she couldn't find it. What she did find was a small rabbit, nearing camp.

Suleima pulled her bow and hit it just as it came into view. Fresh dinner.

"Nice shot. You are getting better with the bow." Gage's praise made her blush. "You are even using it, despite having your powers returned."

"It's a valuable skill," she replied. "I've seen what it is like to be without my powers now. Although it is not a situation I want to repeat, I also don't want to take my powers, or my new skills, for granted."

They worked together to prepare and cook the rabbit before sitting down to eat. "What do we do now?" Gage asked between bites.

"I need to figure out the rest of the spell. There is not much else to translate, just a few words, and then I need to find someone to test it on. If the spell fails to work, it would be a fatal mistake for us all. Our best bet is going to be getting to one of his necromancers. Simply by the nature of what they are and what they do, they have all used some form of the spell that Dirrin has been using.

"If we can capture one and the spell is successful, then we will have some proof it will work on Dirrin. The only thing left after that is figuring out how to get me close enough to Dirrin to perform the spell, but not get anyone else killed in the process," Suleima explained.

"So I am guessing the necromancer needs to be alive for the spell to work?" Gage asked.

"Yep. No ripping out his throat. We have to capture him," she answered.

"You take all of the fun out of it," Gage said, bumping her shoulder with his.

"Yep. No fun. Sorry. Listen Gage, thank you for today. I appreciate your offer to sacrifice yourself, but that was never an option."

"I couldn't just stand by and allow something to happen to you. We need you to finish this battle. You are too important."

"Any person with a talent with the elements could be taught the spell."

"You are important to a lot of people," Gage insisted. "You are important to Dynasira. You are important to all of the people who are willing to go to battle with you. You have become important to members of my pack." He paused a moment, and then changed the subject. "It won't take us nearly as long to trek down the mountain as it did to go up."

They prepared to settle in for the night, and Gage shifted. As he settled next to Suleima, she said quietly, "Members of your pack have become important to me too."

Gage sighed and snuggled a bit closer, resting his muzzle on her shoulder. Suleima was asleep within minutes, her fingers threaded through Gage's fur.

They made it back down the mountain in just a few days, hiked to Suleima's truck, and drove back to the pack house. They stopped and picked up food for every meal on the drive back, tired of eating roasted rabbit, varying types of birds, jerky, and granola.

They reached the pack house late the following day. Kaly came racing out of the house, shouting for Dynasira, who appeared just a few moments later. The two of them bombarded Gage and Suleima with questions before they had even had a chance to get their packs from the car.

Gage stopped them both, raising his hand. "We will fill you both in. We were successful. Details will follow. But I want an update about what happened while we were gone."

Suleima could feel the spells she had put in place before they'd left were still active, though weaker.

"Has anyone seen or heard from Asher or his friends?" Gage asked, referring to the three missing wolves.

"No," Kaly answered. "Not since before you left. There was a rumor they had taken off and left the state, but no one can confirm or deny it."

"We had no direct attacks while you were gone," Dynasira chimed in. "Several came to your cabin, Suleima, but they all took off fairly quickly. Seems the spell you laid worked like a charm. I only saw one group come here to the pack house, but they didn't stay long, and there was no confrontation."

"That is good to hear," Suleima said. "I plan to strengthen and leave the spell I placed on the pack house in place."

"What about your home?" Gage asked, probably already aware of her answer.

"They need to know I am here. They need a target. And I need to find a necromancer. The best way is to have it find me," she replied.

"You can't be serious!" Gage yelled.

"No!" Dynasira shouted at the same time.

"I will put up my wards. I have faced his minions before. I need to finish the translation and complete the preparation for the spell. But we need them to come here. They have to find me. Then I need a guinea pig to try it on," she said, interrupting their arguments. "We need them to continue to think that your pack wants absolutely nothing to do with this fight. If his minions believe it, your pack won't be a target. I will be the only one in their path. We will know exactly where they are headed. It also keeps our numbers against him a mystery. He will have no idea just how many we do or do not have."

"But . . ." Dynasira started.

"No more arguing about it." Suleima held up her hand. "It has been a long couple of weeks. I am tired and ready for some sleep that does not involve a tent. I am sure, Dyna, you will not be far away should I need some help."

"Neither will I," Gage interjected.

"Get some good sleep, Gage. Fill in your pack about everything that happened. I promise, I will be fine tonight." Suleima walked back to her truck and opened the door. When the other truck door opened, she was stunned.

"You know how badly I want details when I climb in this death-trap," Dynasira said, climbing in and buckling up. Suleima was not even fully in the car yet and Dynasira had braced her hands against the door and dashboard.

Suleima laughed. "Just do me a favor and put your hands in the same dents as last time, so I do not accumulate a collection. Thanks." She waved goodbye to Gage and Kaly. It was a very strange feeling, driving away from Gage. This would be the first time in almost three weeks they had not been together. She caught herself glancing at the rear-view mirror until he was completely out of sight.

"So," Dynasira started. "It was a good trip?"

"We accomplished our objective," Suleima responded, pointedly ignoring the insinuation in Dynasira's tone.

Suleima and Dynasira reached the cabin just a short time later. Dynasira followed her into the cabin and helped her unpack, while Suleima removed the spell she had put in place prior to leaving and put up new wards to protect herself before sitting down to have the tea Dynasira had made while waiting for her to finish.

"You have used a bunch of power with the wards and spells today. Are you going to be out of it soon?" Dynasira asked when she sat down, the last of the energy sparkles having dissipated from her ritual.

"Surprisingly, I feel pretty good, but a good night's sleep will help me a lot," Suleima replied. "I will be able to stay awake for a while, so you do not need to rush off."

"So tell me, Suleima, what happened up there on the mountain?"

Suleima told Dynasira the tale of the events that happened while she was away. When she reached the part about the Crystal Dragon, Dynasira was stunned to hear they actually existed.

"What did it look like?" she asked.

"It was very large, a snowy blue color, and its scales seemed to shimmer, though it was blocking most of the light available from the mouth of the cave. The opening seemed to stretch to allow it to fit. It was enormous, probably twice the size of you," she said. "When it grabbed Gage . . . I didn't know if either of us would make it out alive."

"So they are real?" Dynasira asked, dumbfounded.

"They are real. I am not sure if we will ever run into it again, or if there are any others like it, but it was a sight to behold. It even dropped a scale. Gage picked it up and packed it in his bag to show you. I am sure he will show you later." Suleima explained.

"What happened next?" Dynasira asked.

"When it was over, Erist appeared to me. I could hear him and see him. Gage could only see him a bit. It was so strange to see him again, but I've missed him so much. He gave me encouragement. He told me how proud he was of me. He told me I am strong enough to defeat Dirrin, that I always have been, but I now have the tools to do so." She said, "I just hope I can make him proud."

"You can do this. I have never doubted you, and Erist never did either." Dynasira said.

"He faded away too quickly," Suleima said.

"And Gage? What did he think of this journey?" Dynasira asked.

"I am not sure he was terribly thrilled with the whole thing, considering he was the target for most of the things that happened," Suleima said.

"And you said he had fire in his bite?" Dynasira asked.

"Yes, during the fire challenge. The Phoenix forced him to change into a wolf. Neither Gage nor his wolf were in control, and whatever was in control, I assume the Phoenix, attacked me. When he bit my jacket, it caught on fire. When he bit my hand, it was just like being burned with Dirrin's magic."

"Any chance we can repeat the effect? It could come in handy when we face off against the army Dirrin has amassed." Dynasira suggested.

"I don't know. I will have to look into it. Maybe I can find a spell that can replicate it. I have no idea if something like that exists or if it was something only the Phoenix could pull off. And fire has never been my forte, so it could be hit or miss. But he changed in a breath, like you do. Instantaneously. I wonder if I could find something to allow the wolves to change like you. Or even find an explanation as to why they don't."

"Worth looking into," Dynasira said. "I guess I never thought about why Dragons can change like we do, but wolves cannot."

"If I can find something, and Gage is willing to try it, sure. Anything that can help us—I will try." Suleima finished her tea and set it aside. She pulled out every book on magic that she had, setting each on the table. "You said that some of Dirrin's minions came by while I was away. What happened?"

"I stayed out of the way, allowing them to search. The first wave was about five goblins. The second was a banshee, acting as if she was alone. There was a troop of gargoyles keeping watch, but I was careful to stay out of their view. I think they were convinced you were gone, at least for a while, and I didn't see any more visitors after that."

"Thank you for staying here and helping to keep watch over this place and the wolf pack while I was gone. And thank you for always being here to help me. You are the one constant that has been there through all of this chaos. I don't know what I would do without you." Suleima hugged Dynasira.

"You have been there for all of us. I'm happy to be able to repay just a little of that back," Dyna replied. "I'll let you get to work. I will not be far. Call out, if you need anything."

"Hopefully it will be quiet since the last few thought I had abandoned the cabin. I am hoping for a day or two of peace before all of the chaos begins again."

They said their goodbyes and Suleima sat back down at her table, spreading the books out in front of her. She flipped through book after book of spells but came up empty. There was no reference to giving a temporary or permanent alteration to a shifter's natural abilities from any element, let alone specific to fire.

A book of mythology caught her eye, and she flipped it open. She wondered if she would find anything about the elements who revealed themselves to her during her journey. It didn't take long for her to find a reference to the Phoenix.

She skimmed the story, her jaw dropping. Here was the connection! But could she use it to benefit Gage and his wolves?

Chapter 19

The next morning, Suleima woke up refreshed and ready to go. As soon as she made herself some breakfast, so happy she could eat actual food, she got out some of her spell books to finish translating the spell. She was able to decipher the full ingredient list, and everything else was fairly common. There were only a couple of words remaining in the spell, and they both seemed familiar.

By lunchtime, she was ready to get out for some fresh air and a break. She sensed Dynasira in the air, watching over the area.

She headed out of her house and up a trail for a few hundred yards before venturing into the wild of the woods. Using her magical senses more than her sight, she spotted creatures of all sorts running and scurrying through the leaves and resting up in the trees. She had a new appreciation for her senses. Living without them was one of the hardest things she had ever done.

She smiled as she felt a familiar creature attempting to sneak up on her. She walked into the middle of a clearing, luring them into her trap. She lay on the ground, her face up to the sun, giving the illusion her guard was completely down. When the creature slowed and lowered itself to the ground at the edge of the clearing, she knew it was her moment. She opened her eyes to the sky and sunk her fingers into the ground next to her.

With a push of will, a hand emerged from the ground, silently, behind the creature. It reached forward and tugged on its tail, causing the wolf to jump and yelp in surprise.

"Were you never taught not to sneak up on people?" she asked Gage, "It is not polite."

He let out a low growl, bounded over, and sat next to her. She threaded her fingers through the fur at his neck, as she had done so many times on their trip.

"It is so peaceful here," she said. "If I could stay here forever, I could just forget about all of the evil in the world. But alas, it would find me." She felt Kaly in the distance, changing, so she sat and waited in silence with Gage.

"He is glad you were not as complacent as you seemed," Kaly said, emerging a few minutes later from the woods.

"Always alert now. No other choice," Suleima answered.

"Did you have a quiet night?" she asked.

"Yes. I got to sit and talk with Dyna for a while and then rested well, in an actual bed. It was glorious." Suleima smiled.

"Camping not your thing?" Kaly asked.

"I do love a comfortable bed." She turned to fully face Gage. "I found a story last night. It mirrored the story you told me of the first shifter, but it *names* some of the characters in your story. The father of the first werewolf was Volos."

Gage's eyes widened slightly; he must have recognized the name, as she did, from the elements that mentioned it on the mountain.

She nodded and continued, "The woman in the forest was the Dryad. The story I found went into more detail, Gage. The Dryad was Volos's mother. His father was Phoenix. Volos was essentially a volcano, where earth and fire meet.

"The wolf and his pack caught up with his father in the woods. As angry and overcome with grief as the wolf was, he ignored the danger and lunged at his father, intent on killing him. But the Dryad intervened to protect her son. The wolf injured the Dryad when she got in his way, and she cursed him, taking away his access to earth, his ability to shift instantaneously and without pain, dooming all future werewolves to the same fate.

"I thought I saw something behind you in the woods, just before you shifted with the Phoenix. I was about to call out, but it all happened too fast. The Dryad was behind you. They must have worked together to make you shift like you did."

Gage cocked his head.

"What it basically means is that the magic that you use to shift forms is tied to both fire and earth. Your ability to use earth is either gone, or suppressed, which is what makes your shift so different from dragons. I don't know if there is any way to fix that, but Dyna had an idea. And I don't even know if I could manage to pull it off, but I thought, since it applies to you, I should run it by you before doing anything else." Suleima was rambling and stopped abruptly.

Gage bumped his muzzle into her shoulder to prod her along.

"OK!" She laughed. "She wondered if I could find a spell to recreate what the Phoenix did to you." At his growl, she clarified, "Not the taking control, just the fiery bite."

He looked at her.

"You could do that?" Kaly asked the question for Gage.

"I don't know for sure. I would need to create the spell. And fire is not my forte, so there is no guarantee I could pull it off. But if it is something you think you want to try, I could see what I can figure out," Suleima answered.

"He will need to think about it," Kaly replied. "But the idea is intriguing."

"I will do some more research to see if it would even be possible. We can discuss it another time," Suleima said.

"We came out to see if you would like to join the pack for dinner," Kaly started. "Gage has not told us much about your trip up the mountain. Many of us are curious as to what happened, but he said it is your story to tell."

"It is your story as well, Gage," Suleima said, "but I would like to join you for dinner. And the pack of course." She added quickly.

Kaly tried unsuccessfully to hide a smile.

"Tonight then, around dusk, Gage will come and pick you up," Kaly stated. "We will not be eating at the pack house. Gage felt it would be too risky to have everyone come to a house that is supposed to be abandoned. He rented out a local café downtown."

Suleima nodded. "Probably a good assumption. The fewer people in and out, the easier it will be on the spell to keep everything appearing abandoned. Good thinking."

Gage stood and headed into the woods, glancing behind him repeatedly.

"Will you be safe, walking back to your cabin?" Kaly asked. "Or we can walk you, if you can wait for my change."

"I think I will spend a bit more time here, enjoying the peace. Be safe in your travels back, and I will see you later this evening," Suleima answered.

As Kaly walked back into the woods to change again, Suleima stood and headed to the opposite side of the grove. She could feel Gage's gaze on her back as she walked away. She headed toward a small creek that seemed to call to her, keeping an eye on the wolves with her senses. She needed to keep them safe. She needed to keep *him* safe.

When she had spent enough time communing with nature, she headed back to the cabin to prepare for dinner with the wolves. She wanted to do another recharging spell as well as clean up a bit after her hike.

Dynasira was waiting at her cabin when she arrived back and was promptly put to good use, redressing her wounds. The burns were healing well, and she would hopefully be able to leave them open to the air soon to complete the healing process.

"You agreed to go to dinner?" Dynasira asked.

"Yes. Why would I not?" Suleima answered.

"You just spent weeks with the Alpha on the mountain. I just figured maybe you had had enough of the orders." Dynasira laughed.

"No orders. He allowed me to take the lead. Listened when I asked, without much argument."

"Really?"

"Yep. It wouldn't have worked otherwise. He was a huge help, and I never would have completed the trip without him," Suleima replied.

"Sounds like there is something there." Dynasira sat in one of the kitchen chairs. "I want details. You obviously left those out yesterday."

"No details to leave out, although Erist said Gage was a good man, and he approved."

Dynasira roared with laughter. "Good thing I was invited tonight! I have got to see this!"

Dyna had to dodge the kitchen towel Suleima launched in her direction.

It took her longer than usual to pick out her clothes to wear to dinner that night. She finally decided on her favorite black pants, violet top, and her customary black leather jacket. The whole ordeal was a source of great amusement for Dynasira, much to Suleima's chagrin.

As she began her recharging ritual, Dynasira said her goodbyes. She would meet them all at the café in a couple of hours. Suleima completed her ritual and sat back down at her spell books, combing through them to find any other spells in the Old World Tongue, anything to figure out the last few words.

She was so engrossed in her books she never noticed someone approach until the jolt from her wards alerted her. Gage's audible growl was apparent as he crossed the barrier. She had set up her wards as she always had, and had not even thought to allow Gage or his wolves to cross without incident. They could cross, as they wished her no harm, but the jolt they would feel upon crossing was not exactly pleasant.

She was on her feet and at the door in a moment. "I'm so sorry," she said, opening the door wide and pulling down the interior ward so he could pass through. "I got lost in my spell books and . . ."

He touched her arm, stopping her in mid explanation. "It's OK. I'm glad to know you are well protected here. I assume someone who was less friendly would get a more powerful jolt?"

She nodded.

"Then it was worth it to reassure myself you are safe all the way out here on your own," he responded. "Are you about ready for dinner?"

"Yes. Thank you for the invitation," she replied. "Although, the story is also yours to tell. You don't need my presence, or my permission."

He smiled, holding the door open for her to precede him out the door, closing it behind them. "I'd like you to be there." Then added, "For the telling."

She nodded shyly and lowered the ward that had zapped him upon entry so he could walk through without consequence.

He nodded his thanks, opened the door of his car as they reached it, and helped her into her seat, before walking over to get into his own.

The car ride was silent, a comfortable silence, but there was a charge to the air. Suleima watched the trees as they drove through the woods, her senses picking out the creatures waking up as others were snuggling down for the night.

"Rain is coming," Gage stated absently.

Suleima nodded in agreement. "It will be a heavy storm. Lots of rain, lightning, thunder, and wind. We still have a bit before the heaviest stuff gets here, but it is coming."

They arrived at the café a little while later. Everyone was talking and laughing. It had been a long time since Suleima was in a room with a lot of people, and they were all having a good time. Suleima sat silently, absorbing it all, enjoying the ease they all had around one another.

Dynasira arrived fashionably late, as always, and sat down next to Suleima. "You look like you are relaxed and enjoying yourself."

"It has been a long time since we have been able to relax and enjoy time with people we can relate to," Suleima said.

"And no other reason?" Dynasira said, wagging her eyebrows.

"Ha-ha. Very funny," Suleima responded. "I have got to survive the next few battles before I even consider anything more."

"We do not choose when or how things happen. Enjoy your time, enjoy your company, Suleima. We never know that there will be another day," Dynasira said, a melancholy to her voice that had Suleima reach over to place a reassuring hand on her arm.

With Dynasira's arrival, food was ordered and soon the table was full of small conversations and people just enjoying the meal. When the meal was finished, it was almost as if a signal flare had been sent up, allowing for the questions to start.

Questions came from all directions, and Gage quieted them with just a hand gesture. "We will fill you all in on the story, and then you can ask questions as you have them, when we are done." Gage motioned to Suleima. "It is your story to tell."

"You were there too," she replied, but at his continued silence, she gave in and began telling the tale, with Gage adding details and perspective here and there. The wolves and dragon at the table watched and listened to the telling of the story with rapt attention. They wanted more details of the battle with the snake and had many questions about the loss of control Gage had in the battle with the Phoenix. He seemed ashamed of the incident, but his wolves were fully supportive and very impressed with the fiery bite.

"You said you would look into a spell to replicate the bite again for Gage," Kaly started. "Is it something that you would be able to do for more of us?"

Suleima was a bit startled by the question. "If I can find it, and Gage approves, I would be willing to try it out on some of you as well. It could be a great asset and completely unexpected. But I am not even sure it is possible, so it will take time."

"If it works on me, with no unpleasant side effects, then I would be willing to allow it to be used on some of you, if you wish," Gage added.

That seemed to satisfy the rest the wolves, and they were able to continue with the rest of the story of their mountain adventures.

It felt wonderful to have a pleasant and drama-free evening with others. Beyond the stories of their adventures on the mountain, there was no talk of the upcoming battle. It was such a relaxing night, Suleima hated for it to end.

As the dinner party ended and the wolves started to leave, everyone ran to their cars to escape the deluge of rain. Suleima and Gage were soaked by the time they reached his car in the back of the parking lot. As soon as he turned on the car, the windows fogged up and made it impossible to see. Gage quickly turned on the heat to help them dry and to get the windows clear. Suleima assisted with a push of her magic.

"Tonight was nice," Suleima said. "I had a good time. Thank you for inviting me."

"It was very nice. I'm glad you came," Gage responded. "This is a hell of a storm." Gage pulled his car out into traffic, the water on the roads spraying up beside his car because of the water's depth. It took all of his concentration to keep control as the water fought against his car, trying to throw it off the road.

Suleima cracked the window of the car and slid her fingers through the opening, the water running into her palm. Closing her eyes and breathing deeply, she pushed out her will, smoothing the way for the car. She opened her eyes, watching the road.

As they pulled up a slight incline, nearing the turnoff for the pack house, she spoke up, "You can go ahead to the pack house. I will call for

Dynasira, and she can fly me back. The roads near my cabin are likely washed out at this point. I don't want you to get stuck out there."

Gage ignored her and continued driving past the turnoff, heading up into the woods. The roads became rutted, as Suleima suspected they would, but at least they no longer had to worry about the car being swept away by water. When the car bottomed out in even deeper ruts, she did her best to smooth them out with her magic, in hopes of saving them from ripping out vital parts of the mechanics. Even her truck would have had some difficulty getting through the rough terrain. It would have been no match for his car without the use of her magic.

She felt the tree snap and quickly used her gifts with air to block its fall until they were past it, the large tree landing solidly on the road behind them. "Well," she said, "I guess you're going to be stuck with me again tonight. There is no getting over that tree."

Gage grunted but kept his eyes and concentration on the road.

Suleima had closed her window, but she opened it again, curious. This time, she opened it farther, soaking herself again in the process. She held up a hand to stop Gage's protest that the water was filling up his car. Hand and arm out the window, she stretched her senses through the darkness and out into the storm. It was then she felt it. Magic, dark magic. It was fueling the storm. Pushing it, making it rage. And it was directed at her.

Suleima closed the window and looked at Gage. "Someone is out there. This is not just any storm."

Gage looked confused, then enraged. "Who? Where?"

Suleima reached out. She could not feel exactly who it was, but she could pinpoint the location. She gave Gage directions. It was not far from where she usually parked her truck. She could feel the center of the storm there, swirling and churning, being pushed and manipulated. Gage turned up the trail she indicated and slowed down. She was trying to conserve some of her magic to save it for the confrontation she knew was coming, as well as to not alert the person who was pushing it.

He stopped the car where she indicated, and she placed a hand on his arm before he jumped out. "We need to try to capture this person. Not kill them. I think it is a necromancer. I can feel the darkness in the magic."

"A necromancer can control the weather?" he asked.

"They usually start out as shamans. Like me. Something inside them twists though. Like Dirrin. This one must have had a talent with air and water."

"Your eyes are still violet," he said. "I felt you stop using your magic on the ground to level it out."

"I am still using magic, just a much smaller amount. I am keeping us cloaked from the necromancer. It should still think the car is headed to my cabin. If it knew we were heading this way, it might have left."

"Since we do not want to kill this thing, I will stay in human form. I will do my best to subdue it without harming it."

"You can't fight it, Gage. It could and would hit you with a spell before you could get close enough to it."

"Can you cloak me?" he asked.

"Yes, but I need to draw its attention first. Once I do, I'll signal to you. You will have to move quickly. I will need to get to it very fast to bind its powers so it cannot harm you," she answered.

Gage nodded and opened his door when Suleima got out. She pointed in the direction she wanted him to go and walked straight ahead. She knew these woods like no other. She knew she would come out right in the necromancer's line of sight. But when she emerged, she wasn't prepared for what she saw.

A woman stood in the center of the clearing, the wind whipping her hair, despite the fact it was soaked from the rain. The dark cloak she wore whipped around behind her. It was too dark to see, despite the frequent flashes of lightning, but Suleima knew this woman had platinum hair.

"Yanima!" Suleima yelled over the sound of the storm.

The woman's eyes widened as she noticed Suleima standing in the clearing, not far from her. The storm faltered for a moment, but then picked up intensity and aimed directly at Suleima.

Suleima planted her feet to keep from being swept away by the wind and driving rain. Suleima pushed back against the elements being shoved at her. She raised her arm into the rain and pulled. A waterfall of rain fell directly on Yanima's head, knocking her off balance. Suleima felt Gage approach and strengthened the cloaking spell to hide him. She pushed at the wind, shoving it into Yanima's back, knocking her the other way. The key would be keeping her off balance.

Suleima fought for every step she took to get closer. If Gage could get her off of her feet, Yanima would lose her concentration, and she could not instantly recover. Suleima would have just enough time to bind her magic if they could catch her by surprise.

A shot of wind and a blast of water, each from new directions, kept Yanima guessing. Gage was getting close, and Suleima fought the urge to glance at him, knowing the movement could alert Yanima to his presence.

When Gage was within reach, Suleima gave a final gust of wind, hoping Gage could withstand it. It knocked Yanima off balance, and Gage pounced, knocking her to the ground. But Yanima turned and blasted Gage backwards before he was able to pin her down. He flew back about fifty feet and landed hard on his back.

Suleima ignored the urge to run to him, instead liquefying the ground, trapping Yanima's body. She placed a hand on Yanima's forehead, chanting an old binding spell, abruptly stopping her magic and settling the storm down to a rain that was natural. Suleima called forth a vine, using it to bind Yanima's hands as she slowly raised her body from the dirt.

"Nice to see you too, Suleima," Yanima said, the sneer on her face clearly reflected in her tone.

Suleima closed her eyes, pulling at the sound of her voice. Yanima's eyes widened. "I guess I learned some of your tricks," she replied.

Yanima's mouth worked furiously, but no sound emerged.

"Pity. You thought you had the upper hand. You got too cocky. You have bested me too many times before. But I have studied for years to never fall victim to you and your friends again." Suleima sat Yanima up, and then used more vine to bind her legs. She sank her into the ground, enough to cover her hands and legs, so she would not be able to wiggle out of the vines, and then ran to check on Gage.

He was just beginning to stir when Suleima approached him. He grabbed at the back of his head and gasped for air.

Gage blinked up at her and shook his head.

"Relax, Gage." Suleima felt a large knot at the back of his head. "She is no longer a threat. I have bound her magic and taken her voice. Take your time."

He winced as he moved but slowly got to his feet. He stretched, and Suleima could hear the bones in his back snapping and cracking back into alignment.

"Who the hell is she?" he asked.

"We need to get her back to the cabin," she said, pointedly ignoring his question.

Gage let the subject drop. He seized Yanima's arms, and Suleima liquefied the ground. At Suleima's behest, they walked the remaining distance to her cabin through the now light rain. It was a tough and silent walk. Yanima stumbled often, trying to pull out of their grip to get away, but Gage never faltered.

Chapter 20

As they approached the cabin, Suleima lowered her wards for them and called out for Dynasira. She dropped Yanima on her front porch unceremoniously and walked into her house. She moved her spell books out of sight, before heading back out onto the porch. Dynasira was just landing.

"What is going on?" Dynasira asked.

"You remember Yanima?" she replied.

"Glad you are all acquainted. Mind if someone fills me in?" Gage interjected.

"Can you wait out here with her for a minute . . .? And try not to eat her." Suleima motioned for Gage to enter her cabin ahead of her. She poked her head back out the door and added, "I took her voice, so she will not be able to argue back. Sorry."

When inside, she turned to Gage. "I'm really sorry she caused all of this trouble. You'll have to stay here tonight. I will get you set up here soon. You can help yourself to whatever you want to eat."

"Yeah, thanks. But, before we get all settled in, I want some answers. Who is this woman, and what the hell is going on?" he demanded.

Suleima sighed. "It is a long story. Basically, Yanima grew up with a mentor like Erist. Erist and her mentor were friends. She did her best to bully me at every turn. She used to take my voice and perform all sorts of nasty spells on me. She always had a crush on Dirrin. It was no surprise to me to find she had joined up with him when he went on this insane crusade. I know for a fact she has done the same spell as Dirrin to gain magic. I watched her sacrifice a dear friend and absorb his powers. He was a shaman as well as a friend. He was planning to marry Dyna."

"Is she safe out there with Dyna?" Gage asked.

"Dyna is in full control of her emotions when it comes to her. Being able to use her to perform this spell, to make her the catalyst that will allow us to take down Dirrin? It will be her ultimate shame."

"But wait, you were able to bind her powers, and fairly quickly, at that. Without the special crystal and super-secret spell. Can't you just do the same thing to Dirrin?" he asked.

"Maybe once upon a time. After taking all he has from others, I am no match for him," she replied. "It has been a long time since Yanima performed a spell to steal others' powers, otherwise the binding spell never would have worked."

"If she has not performed that spell in a while, then will the spell with the crystal still work on her?" he asked.

"Yes. The way our magic works is we have a well of power to pull from. The spell they used allowed them to steal the wells of others. Therefore, they can hold more magic, perform larger spells, and continue pumping out magic for a longer period of time. A storm like she was conjuring would have drained all of her powers and then some had she not had additional wells to pull from. It would have been a much less powerful storm or a much shorter one. They can still drain their power too far, but it takes them much longer to do so. I, and other shamans like me, must conserve our power, be smart in how we use it. They can be dumb as a box of rocks and spit out power. They also have the option to sacrifice someone to refill and expand their wells almost instantaneously. When my power is drained too low, I perform the Ritual of Alucenia, and I am knocked out for hours afterward. That is a penalty I pay, because I refuse to sacrifice someone else and make them pay the penalty."

"When will you be able to complete the spell?" he asked.

"By tomorrow, we will know if we have a shot at this. If that journey up the mountain was worth it," Suleima answered.

"It was worth it," Gage replied. "I am sure of it." His eyes had a heat she was not used to, and she averted her gaze.

"I need to bind her to the porch. I don't want her in my home, not with my spell books, and I can't risk her figuring out some way to escape," Suleima said.

"I can shift to keep watch tonight," Gage offered.

"Thank you. I'd like to keep you in here. I'll need to recharge. I'll likely be out of commission for several hours at least. I plan to ask Dyna to keep watch out there. She will probably spend most of the night tormenting Yanima, so that will be a bonus." Suleima gathered up what she would need to perform a binding spell and, with a last glance at Gage, left him alone in the cabin to shift.

When she exited the cabin, Dynasira, back in dragon form, had taken position at the edge of the porch. Her snout rested at the top of the steps, blocking Yanima from moving—not that she could, still bound with the vines from the woods. Dynasira lifted her head enough to give a slight nod, indicating she'd heard the conversation inside the cabin. Suleima ignored the waggling of Dynasira's eyebrows.

Suleima placed four rocks as markers on the floor of her porch, creating a box around Yanima. She poured a line of salt between each of the rocks and drew circles around the rocks as well. The rocks would anchor her spell to the earth, the salt acting as a barrier, protecting the anchors as well as creating the boundaries of the spell. She closed her eyes, pulling from her earth power—a weakness of Yanima's—and pushed her will, creating the barrier. She then released the vines holding Yanima's legs but kept her hands bound. "I figured that would make you a bit more comfortable," she said to Yanima. Then she turned to Dynasira. "If she somehow gets out of this, eat her."

Dynasira grinned in response, showing Yanima her very large teeth.

"Thank you, my friend," Suleima said, resting her forehead on the end of Dynasira's large snout. "Without you, I would be lost."

Suleima listened closely, waiting for Gage to finish shifting before heading back into the cabin. She walked over to her kitchen table and again pulled out her spell books, searching through them for the answers she would need to complete the spell. Gage lay at her feet, facing the door of the cabin, his ears twitching on occasion as he listened for anything out of the ordinary.

It was nearly an hour later when Suleima jumped from her chair, startling Gage. She patted him on the head as a quick apology then danced around the room. "I did it!" she yelled. "I figured it out!"

Gage's tail wagged, and his tongue lolled out of his mouth, showing his excitement as best he could.

Suleima stretched and yawned. "I am going to do my recharging spell. The best place for you to wait will be there," she said, pointing to the bed. Her cabin was very small. Suleima gathered all of the items she needed and began to prepare for the ritual. It was hard for her to keep her concentration with Gage laying on her bed, simply watching her. His intense gaze did way more to unnerve her than the unwanted guest out on her front porch. Finally, she blocked out everything but her ritual and completed it.

As the last sparks rained down on her, she stumbled toward the bed. Gage shifted out of the way, making room for her to lie down. She was barely horizontal when she fell into a deep sleep, not even realizing she had snuggled up right next to Gage, her arm draped over his furry body.

He rested his muzzle on her neck, and kept watch at the door, listening for anything to indicate a problem outside.

The next morning, Suleima awoke with the sun. She carefully opened her eyes, making sure she did not move any other muscles and disturb Gage's sleeping wolf. She felt warm and secure. She reached out with her senses and smiled slightly. Dynasira was still lying just off of the porch, and Yanima was still bound to her corner of the porch. She was pacing, but she was not trying to escape.

She became aware of Gage watching her and shifted slightly. "Ready for a new day of fun and adventure?" she asked.

Gage jumped down off the bed, stretching and shaking out his fur. "I will let you shift, and then I will prepare some breakfast before we get started on the spell. You may not want to be close for that. It could be uncomfortable."

Gage growled his response.

"I didn't say you must go," Suleima said. "I just wanted to give you a heads up. Dyna will be here through it all."

Gage turned, and Suleima headed out the door to check on her friend and her prisoner.

"Morning all! How was everyone's night's sleep?" she asked cheerfully. Yanima sat on the ground, narrowing her eyes at Suleima. Dynasira stretched, her scales clicking, before shifting back to her human form.

"I have had better. I was hungry, but you said not to eat her unless she tried to escape. She did not. Only pouted because you took away her voice." Dynasira smiled. "By the way, thank you for that. I enjoyed not having to listen to her at all."

"I will make some breakfast for everyone, when Gage has finished shifting, and then we can get started." Suleima went and sat on the railing of the porch next to where Dynasira stood. She continued, "I figured it out last night. The final piece is in place. I think I can do it now."

"Let's hope this works," Dynasira said. "Then we need to figure out what to do with her in the meantime."

"We need to figure out if this will work or not. Then we will cross that bridge. I am almost afraid to find out if it will work. Everything hinges on this," Suleima replied. "Then, whatever is done with her, we must make sure it stays here. That no one else knows. We can't take the chance of information getting back to Dirrin. Because if he finds a way to prepare for us, *for this*, there is nothing else."

Gage appeared at the door, pulling his shirt over his head. "The pack is not staying at the pack house. I have sent them to stay either at their own homes or with other pack members. We have the room in the basement for wolves who are hurt or out of control. I can keep her there until you determine how and when to turn her over. It is a spelled room. No magic can be used within its walls. I can place a guard, if you think it is necessary, but I don't think she will be able to escape," he said, leaning against the door jamb.

Suleima nodded, "I will come and check it out if we decide that is the best place for her, for now. But first, we should get some food and then see if this actually works."

Suleima walked into the cabin and stoked the fire in her wood stove. She set a pot of water to heat and then began to prepare some toast and eggs for breakfast.

Dynasira came into the house, bringing with her some of the food-stuffs Suleima kept in a root cellar just around the side of her cabin. "How about some potatoes with those eggs? And a bit of the fruit we canned."

"Sounds delicious," Gage said, taking the food from Dynasira and placing it on what little workspace was available in the kitchen area.

The three of them worked quietly, Dynasira and Gage listening to the movements of Yanima outside. Dyna laughed when Yanima got zapped by the barriers keeping her locked on the porch, then headed out to reprimand her.

When breakfast was finished, Suleima made a plate for everyone. She took one out onto the porch; and, creating a small hole, she pushed a plate to Yanima, then sat down with her friends to a quiet breakfast. They ate in companionable silence. Suleima noticed Dynasira kept glancing between Gage and herself, a question written on her face, but thankfully, she never spoke up. Not only did she not want to have a conversation about whatever was happening with Gage in front of him, Yanima was next on the list of people she did not want to share in the conversation with.

She ate silently, trying to ignore the looks from Dynasira and center herself for the upcoming spell. It would not be an easy one, and it would take a lot of her power. She would need to figure out how to conserve power in the battle against Dirrin.

"Gage?" she said in mid thought. "Can you work with me some more? On the stuff you helped me with on our journey?" She glanced at the bow that was just inside the open door of her cabin. "I may need to rely on those skills a bit more before this is all said and done."

He nodded. "We can do that. I will help you with a few other skills if you wish."

Dynasira raised her eyebrows and smiled.

Suleima ignored her. She nodded at Gage, then finished her plate. After getting everything from breakfast cleaned up, Suleima went inside and gathered all of the things she would need to perform the spell. She gathered the ingredients she used for her recharging spell, the crystal, spell books, and a knife.

Using the same vine from the night before, she used her magic to bind Yanima's legs before taking down the barrier spell.

She motioned to Gage to move off the porch. Dynasira stood behind Yanima on the other side of the porch railing, ready to shift and capture if needed. Suleima prepared her hands, just as she would with her recharging spell, closed her eyes, and took a deep breath. "It was not yours, not meant to be. You cannot steal. The power rejects. To its rightful place, it will return. Aided by crimson light and the Flame so true, the power no more belongs to you." Suleima uncovered the crystal she kept hidden within her hands, which began to glow. She heard Gage grunt as the power of the spell worked, but she kept her focus. The crystal grew warm in her hands, then cooled once more, and a cloud seemed to swirl inside the crystal for a moment before it faded away.

Suleima felt a bit lightheaded, having used a good portion of her power. She blinked hard, and looked up at Yanima.

Yanima was white as a sheet. "What have you done to me?" she screamed. It seemed to surprise her when sound came out, but Suleima had dropped the spell that stole her voice when she dropped the barrier.

"I have taken the power you stole when you took Barren's life. It was never yours. Now it is gone, and you will never have access to it again. He is at peace," Suleima said simply.

Dynasira wiped a tear from her cheek and gave Suleima a weak smile.

"Is she OK?" Gage asked.

"She will be." Suleima replaced the barrier to keep Yanima in one area of the porch and headed into the house. Gage followed behind.

"Barren was a good friend. He and Dyna loved each other very much. His sacrifice was a great blow to many of us. To know he could not rest, that his power and essence were trapped inside of Yanima to be used and abused over and over . . . It was a horrible burden for us to carry. I saw his spirit, Gage." He took her hand in his. "He was not as visible as Erist, just a wispy image in his shape and his eyes. He looked right at me and smiled before fading away. He is at peace. I know that.

"I was so happy Yanima was the one we caught. The one we would use as a guinea pig. But seeing Barren . . . There are not words to express how happy it makes me to know he is free now."

"So all of the people Dirrin has killed, those people are trapped within him?" he asked.

"In essence, yes. They are not free as long as their magic is trapped within him," she replied.

"But you saw Erist on the mountain . . ." he started.

"The ritual to steal magic must be started and completed in the moments immediately before and after the death of the person. Dirrin never performed the ritual before killing Erist. I think it is one of the things that makes him so angry with me. He knows I was there that night. He knows Erist deliberately provoked him into acting rashly, attacking faster and more viciously than he would have otherwise, to protect me and keep me hidden. It also kept Dirrin from performing the ritual. Erist had more control over his powers than anyone I have ever known. He could perform spells that would drain anyone else, and it would not even make a dent in his power level."

"Had he stolen powers at some point?" Gage asked. "How could he have a deeper well than anyone else otherwise?"

"I don't believe he ever practiced black magic. He had some way to be able to control the flood of power from his wells. Like my water pump here," she said, beginning to pump the water. "You see how it all floods out of the spout? But, if I place my hand here, blocking most of the water, the water that does come out is more powerful, shoots out farther and with more force and pressure. I believe that is how he was able to do it. By stemming the flood of his magic, he made it more powerful and able to last much longer than anyone else. I just don't know *how* he did it. We never got that far in training."

When she looked up, Dynasira was at her door. She looked as beautiful as ever, but she had been crying. She dried off her hand and walked to Dynasira and embraced her in a tight hug.

"Did you see him, too?" Dynasira whispered.

"You saw him?"

Dynasira nodded and smiled. "He looked good. He is at peace now. I can believe it now." Dynasira's demeanor immediately changed. "Now, what are we going to do with *her*, and how soon can we do it?"

"We need to be smart about this. Until we can decide her punishment, we need to keep her somewhere she can't get away and somewhere there is no chance she will be able to pass on a message to Dirrin to let him know what we have planned. Gage offered his home, the cell beneath, and I think it would be a good place. She must know at this point, or will figure out soon, that the spell I just performed will work on Dirrin and take away his powers. He will no longer be invincible. I will put more barriers around the cell to make sure she is unable to access or use her magic and to keep anyone else from being able to get to her. I can't take the chance she will somehow be able to call a creature to deliver a message to Dirrin," Suleima said. "Also, when it comes to the battle, I will need to work quickly once I have taken his powers. He must not be able to sacrifice more people quickly to regain what he lost. So I will need to distract, enrage, or wound him almost immediately. I need to make sure he can't undo all we have done."

"I will go and get my car. I will meet the two of you back here in a bit. We can load her in, and you can keep her under control until we get to the pack house. I will call Kaly to come and keep guard for now," Gage said, heading out the door and off the porch.

Chapter 21

They got Yanima back to the pack house and secured without incident. Suleima reinforced the spells on the cell. It was a comfortable cell, meant for wolves who had been injured or were out of control but still friends of the pack. There was a mattress on the floor, a clean bathroom, and a door where food and drinks could be slipped inside.

Suleima used a bit of her power to bind Yanima's magic again; so even if she were to find all she needed to recharge her magic, and she got past the wards, her magic would not work. The daggers Yanima fired through her eyes at Suleima almost made her smile.

She met Gage and Kaly at the top of the stairs and explained how to interact with Yanima safely.

Gage walked her out onto the porch.

"I will try to get her out of your cell as soon as possible. Her power has been bound. As long as she is not freed inadvertently, there should not be a problem—and that would be very difficult to do," Suleima answered. "I'm going to go home and see what I can come up with for the fiery bite spell."

"Let me call someone to sit with Kaly, and I can run you home," he said.

"Dyna waited. She can shift and fly me home. You should stay here, help Kaly, and get some rest. It is going to be a tough spell to get through, if I can pull it off. And this battle with Dirrin is likely closer than I would like. The more rest you can store up the better." Suleima jumped off the porch onto the grass. She called to Dynasira, who appeared within moments.

"Wait," Gage yelled before turning and running into the house. He came out a moment later with the pack he had used to trek the mountain, his hand stuffed down into the bottom of the bag, searching for something. After a moment, he pulled out a bandanna and unwrapped the crystal scale that had been dropped inside the cave. "I figured one of you should have this. As cool as it is, I have no real use for it."

Dynasira's jaw hit the floor. "You were serious about the Crystal Dragon? I thought you guys were just embellishing the tale of the trip up the mountain."

Suleima took the scale and held it, feeling a strange vibration within it. "Thank you." She nodded to Dynasira, who shifted, then lifted Suleima in her claw gently. Suleima waved at Gage and closed her eyes to enjoy the flight back to her cabin. She did her best to rest her mind, as she knew the next spell would be difficult, if she was even able to complete it successfully.

She invited Dynasira into the cabin for some tea. Dynasira agreed and sat at the kitchen table while Suleima stoked the fire and heated the water. As a practice, she used her ability with fire to encourage the flames to catch more quickly. She would need to harness power over fire in order to get this spell completed.

While she waited for the water to heat, she prepared the cups, giving Dynasira some quiet time she sensed she needed.

When the kettle whistled, she poured the water and brought it to the table, setting it down before taking her own chair opposite Dynasira. "Are you OK?" she asked.

"Sure," Dynasira said simply.

"I am glad you were able to see Barren, but it can't have been easy," Suleima replied.

"Seeing Barren was hard. I was afraid he was trapped somehow. Knowing he was . . ." She curled her hands into fists and gritted her teeth. "It makes me so angry at her and so sad for him. But knowing he can now be at peace, that means everything to me." She took a sip of her tea. "Thank you. If it was not for you, he would be trapped with her forever."

"Barren was such a sweet man. The way he was abused is unforgivable. I will not allow her to get away with it. She will suffer punishment for her crimes, all of them," Suleima said, determination lending a strange edge to her voice. "He was a friend to me. A great love to you. And no one deserves that kind of treatment."

They finished their tea, and Dynasira stood. "I need to walk for a bit, clear my head. Will you be OK here?"

"Of course. Do what you need. Just please, stay alert. Who knows who our next visitors will be or when they will arrive? While you are gone, I plan to pore over every spell book I have in here to see if I can find a spell for the fiery bite. If not, I need to try to come up with one. It has been a long time since I have created a spell from scratch."

Dynasira headed out the door, and Suleima went to work.

Several hours later, she heard Dynasira roar. Suleima shot to her feet and dashed out the door, reaching out with her senses to find her. She was not far away, only a few hundred yards, and she was hurt. She was surrounded by a group of orcs and goblins. Suleima gathered her powers around her, making sure she was ready to unleash whatever she needed to in order to save her friend.

As she approached the clearing, she slowed, taking in the view. A spear had been shot through Dynasira's wing and several through the meat of her thigh. One spear was through her knee and Dynasira was struggling to stay upright on her injured leg.

Suleima shocked the ground, knocking the orcs and goblins back to give Dynasira room to fight back. She ran forward, whipping the air around Dynasira, pushing the goblins and orcs back even farther.

Dynasira opened her mouth, unleashing a spray of boiling water on the group of orcs and goblins directly in front of her. She swung her tail, batting away the group behind her, so Suleima could use the wind to blow them back into the trees.

Suleima grabbed an orc by the head as she ran past, using her momentum to swing around and break its neck, then charged forward until she was next to Dynasira. She dug her hand into the ground, causing the ground around them to shake, keeping the orcs and goblins off balance, then liquefying the earth so they were stuck. Dynasira let out another spray of boiling water, killing the group of orcs.

Suleima looked around. Most of the creatures were dead, only a few still trapped. She had time to check on Dynasira's injuries before dealing with the few who remained alive. "This will hurt," she said, reaching for the spear through Dynasira's wing. Dynasira roared in pain. Suleima reached for the spears in her legs and repeated the process. "Shift," she said, but Dynasira ignored her. She limped forward to the group of creatures stuck in the dirt and quickly killed them, biting clean through. *Then* she shifted, spitting. "Those are just nasty!" she exclaimed. There was a visible limp to her gait, even after shifting.

"Are you OK?" Suleima asked.

"Nothing vital was hit. Just hurts. I will be OK," Dynasira responded.

Suleima took care of the carcasses that remained before she helped Dynasira walk back to her cabin. Gage was on the way; he was on foot, as a wolf, and headed straight for her cabin. At the rate she and Dynasira were moving, they would get there at about the same time.

She was right. As they emerged from the tree line surrounding her cabin, Gage appeared at the other side. In wolf form and alert for battle, he ran toward them, screeching to a halt right in front of them.

"We are OK. They have been dealt with." She was slightly out of breath from taking Dynasira's weight on the trek through the woods.

Gage growled.

"A few hours and I will be good as new."

Gage looked at Suleima.

"I was not hurt at all," she said. "I went out to help her as soon as I heard her roar." She led them both into the cabin and heated water to clean any injuries.

Gage sat in the center of the room, eyeing the door.

"There is nothing out there, Gage," Dynasira said. "We got them all."

"While you are here, Gage," Suleima said, "I have been working on a spell for your bite."

He turned to look at her.

Suleima walked over to a chair and sat down. "I don't know if it will work. It will not be pleasant to have the spell performed. I don't have any idea how long it could last. You would basically be a guinea pig if you decide you want to try it out. I had to write the spell myself, so it is not a spell someone else has tried before," Suleima said.

Gage walked to her and placed his paw on her hand. He nodded his head.

"When you are ready, we can give it a try."

Gage lowered his paw and sat watching her expectantly.

"Now?" she said startled.

He nodded and waited.

Suleima looked at Dynasira. "What? I want to see this in action too. I am grounded until my wing heals. Watching this will help kill the time, and it'll be entertaining, too," Dynasira interjected.

Suleima was terrified to perform this spell, and something of her feelings must have shown, because Gage settled his chin on her knee and sighed. She threaded her fingers through the fur at his neck and took a deep breath. "If you are sure . . ."

Suleima tried to calm her nerves by taking deep breaths. She needed to be as centered as possible. She rubbed the charcoal in her hands, knelt, and smoothed some of the charcoal along his muzzle. The earth, she held close to her heart, and then sprinkled some in his fur.

She took a deep breath before speaking, "Fire is flame. A bite so fierce. An edge in battle. Fire is passion."

Gage whined as she pushed her will into the spell. She kept hold of the fur at his neck, so he would not run until she was finished with the spell. She dropped a few more small pieces of charcoal on his nose. She looked into his eyes and closed the intention for the spell.

"Did it work?" Dynasira asked.

"Let's go and see," she replied, "I don't want to catch my cabin on fire, so how about we take this test drive out front?" Suleima opened the door for Gage and helped Dynasira to her feet before following him out. He stood just off of the porch.

Suleima threw him a stick, yelling, "Go fetch!"

Gage looked so surprised, he nearly did not go for the stick, but he ended up catching it at the last second. In an instant, the old dry stick smoldered and then burst into flames. Gage dropped the stick and jumped away from the flames that slowly died out as it sat on the damp moss it had landed on.

"Holy shit!" Dynasira exclaimed. "It worked!"

Suleima walked down the porch and approached Gage. He backed away from her. "It is OK, Gage," she said, "You have to bite with the intention to harm for it to actually work." She reached out a hand and touched his muzzle. "It will not hurt if someone touches you."

His tail wagged at her touch.

"Head home, test it a bit on the way. Then shift back. I will meet you later at the pack house. I want to check in and make sure Yanima is secure and behaving herself. We can talk more then. If you run into any problem, come back here or send Kaly," Suleima said. "I want to see if it lasts the whole way back to the house."

Gage nodded, then trotted off into the woods.

"He would follow you around like a puppy," Dynasira observed.

"Stop." Suleima walked back into her cabin.

"Why are you fighting it?" Dynasira asked, following her back in, but showing less of a limp.

"Dirrin is my priority. All of us could die if I don't get this right. I could die regardless."

"All the more reason not to push him away," she replied.

"If you are healed up enough, can you stand guard for a bit? I need to recharge, and it may wipe me out for an hour or so."

"Consider it done," Dynasira said, "but don't think this conversation is over."

Chapter 22

When Suleima awoke, the wind was picking up. A new storm was on the horizon, but when she walked out of her cabin, finding Dynasira on the roof in her dragon form, the leaves in the trees were calm. Suleima listened to the wind she was still hearing. Then looked up to Dynasira, eyes wide.

"The battle is not long from now. Go and gather who you can. Bring them here. I need to find Gage and the other wolves. They are just days away." Suleima ran back into her cabin and grabbed her spell books, ingredients, and the crystal.

Within minutes, she reached her truck and drove it as fast as she could toward the pack house. She did not dare use energy to smooth out the road, so she had to take it a bit slow in areas the storm had washed some of the road away. Luckily, she had used her powers to move the fallen tree when they drove Yanima to the pack house.

She gunned the engine as soon as she reached the pavement and sped off toward the pack house. She was forced to slow again once she reached the dirt driveway that led up to the house, but all in all she made good time.

Gage was emerging onto the porch when she jumped out of her truck. She headed in his direction at a run. He met her halfway, stopping them from falling when she barreled straight into him.

"What is wrong?" he asked, holding her by the shoulders.

"He is headed our way. He and his army are just days away. We need to gather the wolves. Dyna is gathering the rest. It will be a bloodbath if we do not come up with a plan and fast! How did your bite do? Any trouble changing back? Any issues?" Suleima spoke so fast, even her head nearly spun.

"Woah! Slow down a bit. We will be ready for him. We will come up with a plan.

"As for the bite, it was still working when I got back," Gage pointed to a charred piece of something not far from the porch steps. "No difficulty with my change either. I planned to change back in a few hours to see if it was still there," Gage said.

Kaly had come out onto the porch and stood, looking at the two of them in the yard.

"Kaly, has Yanima been behaving herself?" Suleima asked.

"So far. I think she was trying to do something with magic at some point but was getting very frustrated because it was not working," Kaly replied.

"Good to know," she said, then turned back to Gage. "When I was searching for the spell for your bite, I came across a spell that would bind her powers *for good*. It can't be undone. It severs her connection to the elements. I don't feel right making the decision on my own. There is no council or law enforcement for us, and I believe there should be. Right now, morality is the only thing keeping some of us in line. And obviously it is not enough. I can't arbitrarily kill every person who is backing Dirrin. That makes me no better than him. We need some sort of governing body. I know there is no saving Dirrin. If we succeed in this, he will die, but not everyone who follows Dirrin will deserve death."

"I agree," Gage said. "We will need to find a group of us who will be impartial and fair, from a variety of backgrounds and strengths."

"We also need to win this battle first," Kaly interrupted. "I'm sorry, but I overheard what you said when you first arrived. Can you give us all the power you gave to Gage? His bite?"

"I can't give it to all of the wolves. The power it takes would knock me out for days I would be out of commission when Dirrin does show up. We need to see if Gage's bite is the same when he shifts later tonight. If it only lasts for one shift, I may be able to do the spell on Gage and one other, but that will be my limit."

"Let's go inside," Gage said, taking Suleima's hand and leading her. "I will call in the rest of the pack and we'll work on a plan."

Once they sat down and calls had been put out, Gage sat next to Suleima to begin trying to come up with a plan. She pored over spell books, dismissing each one in turn. She landed on the spell Erist used on her and placed her hand over it.

"Can you put some variation in the spell, to make it just different enough he would not be able to sense it?" Kaly asked.

"No. This spell is very specific in its use and how it is performed. It is very powerful in and of itself. Any change made to it would not work at all. Erist wrote it that way," she replied. "What we need is a distraction. Something that will draw his attention. Maybe then I could get close, but it would place a target on someone else."

"If you are so against making someone else the distraction, what if you *were* the distraction?" Kaly interjected.

Gage's eyes were shooting daggers at Kaly, but Suleima was intrigued.

"What do you have in mind?" she asked Kaly.

"Can you astral project or anything like it? Make him see you somewhere you are not? Or make him see something that isn't there, like a large dragon or some other creature, eating you? Taking you off the playing field, or so he would think. If he does not have to worry about you any longer, thinks you are dead, then he would not be looking for you to approach him later," Kaly suggested.

"Projecting visions is not something I could do. But . . . what you said gave me an idea."

"What are you thinking?" Gage asked.

Suleima pulled out the crystal dragon scale. "What if there was a way we could summon him? Just his appearance would be enough of a distraction," she said, the scale glimmering in the light as she tilted it back and forth.

"You want to invite it to join us?" Gage asked incredulously.

Kaly looked very interested.

"He allowed us to leave with the Flame. He knew the Flame would be *used*. It's the only reason anyone would go through all the trouble to get it. So, the cause must be worthy as well. If I can get him here somehow, maybe, just maybe, he would be willing to help us. Even if he didn't participate in the actual battle.

"Crystal dragons are thought to be a myth, even by the Dragon Clans. For one to appear in the midst of the battle? It would shock everyone, Dirrin included. That may be enough to get me close to him. If the Crystal Dragon would fight along with us . . .? Any addition to our numbers would be spectacular," Suleima continued.

"How do you propose we summon this thing?" Gage asked.

"Scales are magical. They can be used for all types of spells. They are also very valuable. If I send it back to him with a note asking nicely, maybe, just maybe, he'll show?"

"You could hold onto the scale and send him a note saying you have it," Gage suggested.

"That would come off as hostile, and I don't want to have any interaction with him start out that way. This has to be on his terms or not at all. I can't blackmail him. I'll ask nicely and see if that works. If not, then I'll come up with a new idea."

Suleima walked out onto the deck and pulled with her powers, summoning an eagle to her side. There was no way a smaller bird would be able to carry a scale the size of the Crystal Dragon's. She sent it off with a push of will and hoped the eagle would get to the dragon in time and the dragon would answer her request.

"That bird can get to the mountain, but Dyna could not have flown you up to the top?" Gage asked.

"The eagle is not trying to get the Flame. I had to perform the tests for any of the paths to show up. There is no shortcut. You must complete the tests before you can be shown the Flame," Suleima answered.

"How long do you propose we wait to find out the dragon's answer?" Gage asked, clearly not liking the idea. But, then again, his last interaction with the dragon was not so pleasant. Being nearly torn in half would not have sat well with most people.

"Clearly, time is not on our side. We need to come up with a plan B for several reasons. The dragon may not show; the dragon may refuse to help. If he does show, the dragon could fail to be the distraction we hope for," Suleima explained. "We need to be ready for anything, because if we fail at this, it would be fatal to us all."

"Can a shaman like Dirrin heal himself?" Kaly asked.

"Dirrin had a small talent for healing at one time. But he never cared enough for anyone else to put in the effort to learn. As far as I know, he can't. But I gravely injured him in our last battle. He may have nurtured a talent to heal himself," Suleima responded. "But even if he has, it is not instantaneous. Any injury would slow him down."

"Then we can hurt him without using magic?" Kaly asked.

"In theory, yes. But we would have to be close enough to inflict damage. He can't see the attack coming. He could use his powers to shield himself, or deflect the attack elsewhere," Suleima answered.

"Then we need to work with the bow. He won't expect you to have those skills," Gage said. "We can go while there is still some light." Gage stood and walked out to the garage.

When Gage reemerged, he was carrying a lightweight bow and a quiver with metal arrows.

Gage set the weapon on the porch at Suleima's feet. "These arrows are more accurate than the ones we carved on the mountain. And I figure they will be harder for him to melt than the wooden ones would be for him to set on fire."

Suleima nodded and lifted the bow, weighing it in her hands. She pulled back on the string and tested it. It felt natural in her hands. Gage reached for her and she took his hand, allowing him to guide her off the porch and around to the back of the house where there were a few well-worn targets set up.

Gage dropped her hand and pointed at three of the targets. "These targets are stationary. Your targets will not be. Most likely, you will also be on the move. For now, shoot at each of these targets, in differing order, while moving. I want you to shoot at a different angle for each shot. You got pretty good with your aim when up on that mountain. Refresh your muscle memory. Get used to the new bow, its weight, and the weight of the arrows. They will all be different than the bow you shot up on the mountain, but you will carry this one with you into this fight."

She was three arrows into her practice when she felt it. Something was coming.

She opened her senses and felt the band of orcs and goblins, twenty strong, heading for the pack house. She pulled at the ground where she felt them, the earth rolling beneath their feet, slowing them down and causing them to stumble.

Gage shouted for the few wolves that were around, and she sensed Kaly as she came back out of the house and headed in their direction. Most of the wolves were still in human form, but a few had been keeping watch near the property and caught up to her and Gage, passing them by in blurs of fur.

When the first of the orcs was in range, Suleima fired an arrow, nailing it in the shoulder, its cry of pain cut short as a wolf ripped its throat out on the way to the next orc in the group. Suleima let loose another arrow, but it went wide of her target. She pulled with air, pushing the arrow farther and faster at a goblin instead, hitting it in the throat, dropping it instantly.

Gage, Kaly, and another wolf still in human form waded into a group of goblins, fighting them back in hand-to-hand combat. Suleima was impressed. They all seemed well trained, and they moved in such a synchronized fashion; they must have trained together often. She fired off a few more arrows, using air to redirect the ones that missed even while she continued to pull at the earth to slow down the flow of creatures heading in their direction.

Several wolves came from the direction of the road. They must have been guarding the road leading up to the pack house. Those wolves dove into the middle of the fray, seamlessly blending in with the other fighters in the pack in human form.

Suleima scanned the area, but all the creatures seemed to be coming from the same direction. There was only one outlier, and she headed straight for it. Pulling from earth, she tangled the gargoyle up in the tree when it would have tried to fly away, wrapping branches and vines around its arms, legs, and wings. She could hear its frustrated scream over the din of the fight going on behind her. Slowly wrapping and pulling, re-wrapping and dragging, she pulled the gargoyle down from the highest branches of the tree to the lowest. It screeched in anger as she closed the distance, fighting to free itself. She pulled back the last arrow and released it. It burrowed into the gargoyle's eye, whose flailing abruptly stopped.

She took a long, deep breath, scanning to make sure she hadn't missed anything. Finding that the wolves had taken care of the remaining creatures, Suleima released the gargoyle from the tree and dragged it back to the pile the wolves had already begun assembling.

Gage met her halfway.

"They obviously know that we are here and working together now. I'm going to reset the wards surrounding the pack house. I will not leave you and the pack without a barrier to protect you. It will also alert both you and me, in the event something tries to break through."

Gage nodded, then looked her over. "I'll pull the pack into the house until you have completed what you need to do. Is there anything I can get for you? You weren't hurt, were you?"

"No. Are your wolves injured?"

"A few scrapes and scratches that will be healed by nightfall." He paused, taking in the defeated look she knew she wasn't hiding well and took her hand in his. "We defeated them this time. We will do it again." The conviction in his voice almost made her smile.

"I've known this was coming. I've known that I could not avoid it, no matter how much I wanted to. I just . . ."

"What?" he asked, when she didn't continue.

"I don't want to lose anyone else."

Gage hugged her tightly, then bent to look directly into her eyes. "I've seen all that you have done to keep me and my pack safe. I just watched you shoot a quiver full of arrows and take down hellish creatures who are bound and determined to take everyone out who isn't with them. Everything you have done has been to give us all a chance in the fight that is inevitable. This fight would have eventually come here, even if we hadn't been *lucky* enough for you to choose here to settle and heal." He took her hand again. "We have knowledge of the enemy and a weapon to fight him, because of you. We have a chance to survive, *because of you*."

Suleima took a deep breath and squeezed his hand. "Thank you. I need to stay out of my head and keep pressing on." She handed him her quiver and bow. "Take your pack inside. I'll let you know when I am done. Then we can dispose of the trash and practice some more. I missed too many shots and had to use magic to correct the trajectory."

Some time later, Suleima's arms felt like dead weight, so Gage relented and let her take a break, though he was clear to say "For now," before they packed everything up. She had gotten fairly good at hitting the targets, at least until her arms got too tired, and then she felt like she couldn't hit a dragon a foot in front of her.

As they rounded the house, she saw all of the pack, at least all of those who would be participating in the battle. They stood expectantly, waiting for orders from their Alpha. As he stepped forward to speak, Suleima placed her hand on his arm. She felt several of the wolves bristle at her touch and unspoken command of their Alpha, but nothing was said.

A loud screech, followed by a roar, announced the incoming dragons before Suleima could speak. The wolves all went on alert but calmed at a gesture from Gage. Suleima turned to face the incoming dragons and the rest of the shamans who were along for the ride. Although they would not fight at her side, they would be immensely helpful if any of the wolves or dragons were injured.

Dynasira shifted the moment her talons hit the ground, while the other dragons stayed in their dragon form. She walked forward, meeting Suleima halfway. "We have got all we are going to get. The jinn are coming by car and will be here in a few hours. Several of the dragons took their sweet time, but they will be here soon as well. The thunderbirds are with them. With only us and a few wolves, we'll need every advantage we can get."

"I really hoped for more, but what we have will have to be enough. I hope this is a short fight. A drawn-out battle will be devastating for all of us," Suleima replied.

Gage approached them. "We will shift tonight, to go on a hunt and practice our fighting skills. We invite you and the other dragons to observe or participate as you wish, so we can learn from each other and become familiar with working together."

Dynasira nodded, "I think it would be a wise idea. We can't risk getting in each other's way out there. We do not wish any of those on our side getting caught in the crossfire. It would also be wise for you and your wolves to see our skills, as each clan is unique. Your wolves will need to familiarize themselves with what the acid from the Verana clan looks like, as it is toxic for a while after it has landed. A wolf running through it would be injured."

"We could also use it to our advantage if we are being chased," Gage surmised. "If they follow us through it, while we avoid touching it . . . yes, a great asset to learn each other's strengths."

"You must avoid the black dragons at all cost, Gage," Dynasira said. "You and your wolves. They are *not* on our side. They are the dragons of death. Their venom is deadly. It is instantaneous, and they can spit or secrete that venom."

"Black dragons bad. Got it," Gage said. "We will be happy to let you handle those."

Dynasira took in the bow Suleima held to her side. "Learning new skills, are we?" she asked.

"Working on improving skills Gage taught me on the mountain. We are going to need all the help we can get, and every surprise is a mark in our favor. We are hugely outnumbered. Only working together will we be able to do this."

They were heading back to the house when Suleima heard a familiar boom of thunder. The thunderbirds were on their approach. The dragons shifted to give room to the enormous birds that landed. They were nearly the size of the dragons with wickedly sharp beaks and sharp talons. They had been instrumental in taking down the cyclops in the previous battle, and she hoped they would be able to help once more to take out that horrible beast.

Chapter 23

As the last of the members of their small army descended, the wolves prepared to shift. Kaly shifted last, waiting until Gage was fully in wolf form to communicate to Suleima that indeed, his fiery bite was gone. She nodded in response, then watched as Kaly headed off to change herself.

Gage approached her and sat down at her right. Suleima knelt. "I will only be able to do the spell to you and one other wolf before the big battle. You will both need to stay in wolf form for the entire battle, unless you are willing to give up the fiery advantage. You need to choose which wolf ahead of time and let me know."

He nodded solemnly in response.

The wolves, thunderbirds, and dragons went out into the woods to hunt and practice maneuvering together. Suleima waited back at the house, checked the wards on the cell where Yanima was being held, and greeted the jinn as they arrived by car.

"Hamanad," Suleima said, addressing the leader of the jinn. "Welcome. Thank you for coming again to face off against Dirrin. Your healing will be valuable, as we are very outnumbered."

"We can't allow a man like Dirrin to destroy the world as we know it," he replied.

"I must ask you, Hamanad," Suleima started, "Dirrin's necromancers have brought back several of the creatures we have defeated in the past, specifically the cyclops, ent, and Jorogumo. With your powers, are you able to disrupt the connection of the necromancers to these creatures? And, if we can do that, will it send those creatures back where they came from?"

"We can help with that, at least some of us, but we would need to get close to the necromancer. It would not kill or destroy the creature immediately, but it would weaken it, making it easier for others to take it down," he answered.

"We will need to share that with the others when they come back from the hunt." Suleima turned to head back to the porch when she felt the disturbance of the ward she'd placed on the pack property. It was coming from the opposite direction than the others had gone hunting. She could sense at least twenty creatures, as they fanned out, attacking the wards in several places trying to bring them down. Gage would feel the attack as well.

She directed Hamanad to get himself, the rest of the jinn, and the other shamans close to the house to prepare to handle any injuries, and then she ran toward the group attacking the ward near the road. Suleima pushed at the wards, strengthening them to delay the creatures from getting through. There were four goblins at the location she approached, and she could sense at least five more groups of equal size spreading out around the boundary. She sensed the dragons, wolves, and thunderbirds all returning to the pack property quickly.

Suleima pushed and pulled at the earth below the goblins on the other side of the ward from her, causing a small earthquake which opened a fissure beneath them. Two of them fell inside and she snapped the fissure closed, crushing and burying them. Then she liquefied the ground, burying one to its knees, the other to its hips and raced past the ward barrier. Pulling the knife Gage had given her on the mountain, she sliced the throat of one and then threw the knife, using air to guide the trajectory and impaled the last goblin in the eye.

An orc appeared at her side, tackling her to the ground. Suleima's thick leather jacket provided some protection from its sharp claws as it raked at her. She pulled an air vacuum and surrounded the orc with it, sucking all of the air from its lungs and the area around it. The orc released her, clawing at its own throat, trying to get air. Suleima wedged her knees between her chest and the orc, shoving it off her and diving for her knife. Her hand had just closed on the hilt when the orc's hand wrapped around her ankle, yanking her back painfully.

Without warning, the orc was wrenched into the air, dropping Suleima's ankle in surprise, as a thunderbird lifted it into the air before pulling it in two with its talons.

Suleima stood, testing the ankle with her weight—sore but not severely injured. She sensed the wolves, dragons, and other thunderbirds in the distance, each working together, taking out the groups surrounding the wards. Suleima headed in the direction of a group mixed with both orcs and goblins. She took off at a run, as she felt Dynasira heading for them, as well as a group of wolves from another direction.

They were on a collision course.

Suleima used her power to increase her speed. The wolves were nearly on the group when Dynasira opened her mouth. Suleima pulled dirt and water from the ground, throwing it into the air and packing it like a shield, directing the boiling water up and over the wolves as they converged on the group below.

The wolves took out the orcs and goblins easily, as Dynasira landed and shifted to human form next to Suleima. Her head bowed. "I didn't see you coming. I wouldn't have harmed you."

"No harm was intended, no harm inflicted. We must get used to fighting alongside one another." Suleima stood blocking Dynasira from the wolves.

One of the wolves approached, snapping its jaws in Dynasira's direction, while most of the other wolves took a defensive stance, watching Dynasira warily. One wolf, a honey color with gold-tinged brown eyes, moved to stand between its packmates and Suleima. The sneer of the wolf was clearly visible, but no sound emerged. Kaly.

The wolves warily kept Dynasira in sight as they backed away, heading for the porch, where the rest of the pack were gathered. The dragons and thunderbirds were overhead, scouting for any other creatures, but Suleima couldn't sense any others close by. She felt the wolves shift back to human.

"I apologize, Suleima," Dynasira stated. "I never saw them approach. I was too focused on my prey. If you had not come . . ."

"We must all be more vigilant, Dyna. We are fighting alongside a group of people who are new to us. We are as unfamiliar with their fighting styles as they are to ours. I know there was no intention to harm, and I am glad I was there." Suleima headed toward the ward, pulling Dynasira with her. The two of them gathered the remains to be disposed of, and as the other dragons and thunderbirds finished scouting the area, they joined in, making quick work of the cleanup.

By the time Gage and Kaly emerged from the house, both in human form, the creatures had been piled at the road. "I've heard from the wolves what happened."

"I apologize, Alpha. It was not my intention to harm any of the wolves. I will be much more careful in the future." Dynasira said, bowing her head in capitulation.

"No one was harmed. It will take time. That's why we were all out together tonight. One time won't make us perfect—we just need to stay vigilant and aware."

Dynasira nodded her agreement.

No more was said, as Suleima bent to take care of the pile of bodies. Smoke obscured the pile, and when the rain washed away the smoke, the bodies had been absorbed into the ground in the form of dust. Nothing remaining to be reanimated and used again.

She spun at a loud roar. Chills ran down her spine.

The Crystal Dragon careened into the yard, landing just feet from Suleima, and snarled. "I am here. What do you want?"

Suleima could hear the commotion from the wolves and dragons who had come running when they heard the roar, but she tried her best to tune them out. "I really appreciate your coming here. I have called you here to ask you for a favor."

"A favor? A favor! You called me here because you want something from me?" he yelled.

Suleima nodded. "I passed your tests. I was deemed worthy of the Flame, and Erist told me I was the only one who had a chance to destroy the army that is headed this way with a goal of annihilating everything in its path. The Flame is used to keep the balance. As the keeper of the Flame, I imagine it is your duty to help to maintain that balance. We are sorely outnumbered, and I must get close enough to Dirrin to perform the spell, using the Flame." As her other arguments did not seem to be having any effect, it was time to try to stroke his ego. "I do not think there is any creature on this planet that could capture attention like you. An actual crystal dragon, the myth confirmed."

The dragon actually laughed. "Clever girl. The army that comes your way is close." He looked around, taking in the ragtag bunch of people and creatures. "You will be far outnumbered, but you are the last to stand against him." He walked around in a circle, then crouched down on his paws, bringing his snout down to Suleima's level. "Pure of heart, you are, to earn the Flame, there is no other way. Brave, you are, taking on a group so much more powerful, after nearly being killed by that same group last time." He paused, and Suleima was not sure he would continue. "I admire your guts. I will help. The balance must be restored."

Waking up to a tent city surrounding the pack house was a strange sight to see.

Dirrin and his goons were only a few hours away, she could feel it. They would need to gather their forces and move, meeting them away from the pack house, but before they left, she needed to find Gage.

Gage was opening the door to the house, as she stepped up onto the porch. "It will happen today, so we must get moving. But, before we do, I need your decision. Who else will get the ability to bite with fire?" she asked.

"Kaly," he answered simply.

"Excuse the interruption." The voice belonged to the Crystal Dragon, but he was in human form. Platinum white hair, blue eyes so light they were almost white. His skin shimmered, as if the iridescence of his scales could not be fully hidden. "But what exactly do you mean?"

"The Phoenix gave Gage a bite that caught things on fire, during our challenge with him. I created a spell which will allow that same ability, during a single shift. I can't create the ability for every wolf, but I should have the power to do it for two of them."

"Why can you not do it for more?" he asked.

"I need a lot of my power to perform the spell on Dirrin," she said.

"I am aware, but the spell to add fire to their bite should be a simple one," he replied.

"It is fairly simple, but I am not strong in fire," she said. "I do not know what other spells I will need to perform, and I can't run my power too low. If I do that, then I will be useless," she responded.

"Did Erist never teach you to siphon your power?"

"He was killed before he could teach those skills to me. I taught myself the rest."

The Crystal Dragon's human form closed his eyes and backed up a step. Raising his arm, he pointed behind her.

She turned, finding Erist's figure flickering behind her.

"My child, to see you again, on the cusp of this battle. I couldn't be happier with you and how you have honed your skills. I'm here to help you. I can't physically battle with you, but I can help to give you the boost you need, to strengthen your friends, and help them survive this grueling battle. I know each and every death will weigh on you, as mine has. Although that weight should not lay on your shoulders."

Suleima blinked away tears, "If I was stronger . . ."

"Then we would both be dead," he interrupted. "It has happened just as it should. I'll help you as much as I am able. Now, close your eyes child and pull from your power, as when you first began."

Suleima closed her eyes and gathered a small amount of power in her hands. When she opened her eyes, she held a small orb in her hands, like those she conjured when recharging.

"Yes, my child. Just like that. Now compress the orb. Make it smaller."

She did as he asked.

"Now let it expand until it is done. Allow it to tell you how far it can go, do not limit it."

The orb expanded, and Gage stepped back through the doorway into the house, as the orb took up much of the porch.

"Now pull it into orbs, the same size as you were taught."

The orbs slowly pulled away from the center, each floating. There had to be more than thirty. Suleima's eyes grew wide.

"Each of those orbs contains the power of your first. You explained it well, when you spoke to Gage at your cabin. If you increase the pressure, you can get a blast from only a trickle. It will take practice, but you have the power you need to help all of the wolves who fight at your side. The spell using the Flame will still deplete most of your well. You must use your remaining power wisely until you can recharge. But your new tricks"—he smiled at her—"those will come in handy I am sure. Good luck, my child. I know you will do all you can. You're stronger than you have ever believed. Know that."

In the next breath, he was gone. The Crystal Dragon stood just off of the porch.

"How are you able to bring Erist here?"

"Erist was a great shaman, a champion for the balance in this world. He tied himself to the mountain, so in the event of his death, he could live on in spirit as a protector of this place. The cunning old man always knew more than he let on about things that had not yet come to pass. In tying himself to the mountain, he is also tied to me, as guardian of Mount Lucent.

"The wolves will need to shift soon. Once done, perform your spell as quickly as possible, then recharge. We need to get moving." He nodded to her before turning and walking away.

Gage handed Suleima the bow and arrows she had used the night before, and the knife he had given her to carry on the mountain. Their hands lingered for just a moment. "I'll go fill them in. We'll all be out, in wolf form, for you to work your magic on. Get everyone else ready, while you wait on us." He reached up a hand, touching her face. "I'll see you in a bit."

Suleima's heart tightened. She knew how heartbroken Gage would be if any of his wolves were hurt or killed. How heartbroken she would be.

Suleima prepared the rest of the group for leaving, and they were all ready and waiting when the wolves emerged. Suleima walked to Gage and pulled out her charcoal. She repeated her spell, taking her time and pulling her power as Erist had explained. Each wolf received a push of will, beginning with Gage. He moved and stood with each wolf again, keeping them centered and under control with the jolt they would feel with the spell. Suleima was still surprised when it was all said and done, by how energized she felt.

She performed her recharging spell to top off her power as the wolves tested their new bites on anything they could find. "Remember," she warned, "if you shift, the bite will be gone, and I won't be able to redo the spell in the middle of all of that chaos."

With that last warning, they all headed to find Dirrin.

<h1 style="text-align:center">Chapter 24</h1>

She had dropped her glamour to conserve her power, but she felt self-conscious and continually pulled her hair down to cover the left side of her face when the wind blew it away. Gage alternated between walking with his pack and walking with Suleima. He bumped her leg if he saw her messing with her hair and covering her face.

The forest around them seemed unnaturally calm. Very few woodland creatures scurried about, and the footsteps of only a few in her very small army were audible. The forest seemed to be holding its breath, waiting for the battle that it sensed on the horizon.

Suleima picked up her pace, moving to the front of the group as she felt them near a clearing. Dirrin was in there with all of his minions, and the battle was at hand.

She turned when she reached the front and motioned for everyone to stop. The clearing lay just past the cluster of trees in front of her, blocking her view, but she could feel the enormity of the forces that were hidden ahead. She fought to keep her composure as anxiety threatened to freeze her in place. There was only one choice she could make here.

The next moment, she spun, drawing her bow and firing an arrow at a gargoyle that leapt out of a tree at her. An orc followed close behind, and one of the werewolves ripped his throat out and his corpse was lit on fire.

Everyone went into action. The Crystal Dragon joined her, the other dragons shifted and took flight, and the shamans set up a protective barrier which would house the makeshift hospital tent. The wolves shot ahead, taking out the smaller creatures as they emerged into the woods.

A sound drew Suleima's attention. The ground shook with each step the cyclops took. A huge club swung back and forth, knocking over trees, foes, and allies alike. Suleima drew the attention of the jinn and shouted as one of the Amarola dragons was already in motion. Moving in, it lifted a jinn, carrying him to find the necromancer controlling the cyclops.

Two thunderbirds dove at the cyclops, each taking turns to dive for his eye while avoiding the swing of the club.

While the thunderbirds attacked from above, a group of four wolves fought in unison, one jumping in to bite at the cyclops's legs and ankles, causing burns and tearing at muscles and ligaments and then jumping back out of reach while another took its place. They seemed to be dancing. The coordinated attack was no more than an annoyance to the cyclops, who kicked or swung his club like swatting at bothersome flies. The cyclops roared as the claws of the enormous thunderbirds raked his arms, leaving long gashes, but his grip on the club never loosened.

Time seemed to stand still as the cyclops's club connected with the head of one of the wolves with a sickening sound. It dropped like a rock, and an echo of howls erupted from the pack. No more than a second later, Gage and Kaly's wolves came into view. Kaly grabbed the wolf by the scruff, dragging him away from the battle scene, and Gage took up the fourth spot in the dance with the cyclops. Suleima held her breath. The club came dangerously close to hitting Gage. She uprooted a tree and deflected the blow.

The cyclops knocked one of the thunderbirds to the ground with its club. Three of Gage's wolves bit at the cyclops's ankle as it moved to crush the thunderbird with its foot. The pain caused him to misstep, missing the thunderbird by a few feet.

The last remaining thunderbird dove. As the club came up, Suleima pulled at the closest tree with her powers, wrapping a branch around the cyclops's arm, preventing it from being able to swing the club any farther. The thunderbird ripped the cyclops's eye out of the socket. The cyclops roared in pain. Conscious of the amount of energy she expelled with each pull of her magic, she didn't dare use more on the cyclops. With more battles to fight before even reaching Dirrin, she would need to rely on her allies, as much as it pained her to put them in harm's way.

The wolves continued to bite at the cyclops, as it yanked at the branch still trapping its hand. It pulled at the tree branches, ripping them from the trunk of the tree, swinging at everything and nothing. It could no longer see, but the strength behind those blows would kill anything it hit. The swinging kept the wolves too far away for them to be of any use, and they switched to the smaller targets of orcs and goblins to thin the herd of Dirrin's minions as much as possible. The more dead minions, the fewer resources for Dirrin to sacrifice to regain power if Suleima's spell worked.

Suleima fired metal arrows at the cyclops as fast as she could, several of them sticking out of his arms and chest. As the Amarola dragon returned with the jinn, it let out a screech, and Suleima and the wolves moved as far out of range as they could. The dragon released a flurry of lightning, knocking the cyclops to its knees. The arrows conducted the electricity. The cyclops convulsed violently and roared in pain. As the spasms faded, a few wolves took their chance, ripping out the cyclops's throat. The jinn dropped to the ground near the downed thunderbird to heal it, while three wolves closed ranks, protecting the fallen thunderbird again.

Suleima could hear the rage of battle above her but could not see the dragons in the sky. She had yet to see the black dragons during this fight, but she had seen enough of them in previous battles that she was not eager to see them again. She tried to block out the sounds of the battle above and concentrate on the battle coming her way. It was not even close to being over yet.

The ground shook again, the trees swaying out of the way as the ent came to join the fray. The large tree-like being lumbered through the forest, knocking down saplings, and any of Dirrin's creatures that didn't move fast enough, in its path. One of the Rojada dragons flew overhead with a jinn in its talons. She watched it drop and could barely make out a figure in the distance near the landing spot. She sensed the magic he was wielding and knew he was the one responsible for the ent. The colors of the magic were vivid to her eyes. She watched as the magic the jinn wove disrupted the necromancer's spells. He turned quickly to run away, but was halted by the wolf, dropped in by a thunderbird. In the chaos of it all, Suleima appreciated the way her ragtag bunch of soldiers were working together. But soon, her eyes were drawn back to the battle raging in front of her.

More wolves converged on the ent, abandoning the rapidly thinning goblin and orc herds to help with the much larger target. Several of the wolves showed signs of injury, however, not a single wolf was showing signs of slowing down in their pursuit of any of the targets of battle. A group of wolves, led by Gage, bit at anything they could reach on the ent, jumping back and out of the way after each bite, trying to stay out of its grasp in a dance reminiscent of the battle with the cyclops, but so much more intricate, as there were at least ten wolves from the pack surrounding the ent, and the ent had many vines, reaching out to grasp at anything that got in its way.

A light brown wolf was not fast enough and got caught in a thick vine that reached out, pulling it in close to the ent, constricting around the wolf.

Unable to stomach the idea of another wolf from Gage's pack being killed, Suleima desperately pulled at her fire magic. There was a small bit of smoldering on the vine, near the wolf, from one of its bites. Suleima pushed air at it so it grew in size and intensity. The wolf fell from its grasp, unconscious, but alive. A jinn ran in, dragging the wolf out of harm's way before healing it. A Rojada dragon lit up the top half of the ent with bright orange flames, while Suleima pushed at a few more of the smoldering pieces the wolves had inflicted, turning it into an inferno. The ent let out a blood-chilling squeal that halted nearly all action, engulfed in the flames.

Its limbs crackling, bark splitting away, the flames raced to eat the soft tissues under the bark.

The largest remaining thunderbird swooped in, ramming its huge talons into the back of the burning ent, sending it careening into the forest floor. There, its movements slowed and stopped. A dragon from Clan Azula, smaller than Dynasira with scales slightly more muted in color, swept down and extinguished the remaining flames.

Two reanimated monsters down. One to go.

Suleima scanned the edge of the tree line for movement. Several of the wolves were back to taking out orcs and goblins, thinning their herds further. It was when she saw the wolves hesitate that she first saw it. The Jorogumo. Not only was she as beautiful as before, but she looked deadlier still. Jet-black hair hung to her waist, a skintight black bodice covered her, and then flowed out in a floor length black skirt with a high slit, exposing her leg with every other step. She looked ready for a ball, completely out of place in the middle of a raging battle in the woods. Her eyes carried an eerie glow, which was not there before the necromancers brought her back.

And she was not alone. She had four escorts. The three wolves who had disappeared from Gage's pack, and a fourth, who affected Kaly so much her reaction stood out on the battlefield. It must be the wolf who attacked Kaly, causing the injury to her throat.

Suleima signaled to the jinn and called for Dynasira to give one of them a ride to search for the necromancer controlling the Jorogumo. She shouted a warning at Gage and ran forward to do what she could to help.

A thunderbird screeched, diving at the Jorogumo, snatching at her hair and lifting her off the ground. She shifted in response and bit the thunderbird's talon, causing him to drop her. He nearly dropped to the ground from the fast-acting poison but was scooped up by a second thunderbird and flown back toward the shaman healers. Gage howled and snapped his jaws at her, drawing her attention away from a wolf who was getting closer.

The black wolf who had left the pack, Asher, lunged at Kaly, who was approaching from the side, but never expected the bite he received when she turned. He was able to grab some of the fur at her neck, but he was unable to do any damage. The two wolves with Asher hesitated, but the fourth wolf, a deep brown coat on him, attempted to flank Kaly. She turned, jumping back out of the way. She almost seemed as if she was going to cower, but her hair rose on end and Suleima could see the snarl, even if no sound emerged. She snapped her jaws at him—a challenge—and then sat back on her haunches, almost looking . . . bored.

He snarled and leapt in her direction, but Kaly charged the brown wolf, slamming her shoulder into his front legs, knocking him off balance, and then spun, grabbing him by the throat and shaking her head violently. The fur and tissue surrounding Kaly's jaws smoldered before bursting into flame, and the wolf let out a sickening howl. She finally let go, tossing the carcass away from the fray before turning back to help the rest of her pack with the Jorogumo. Asher and his buddies were blocking her path. Two of Gage's wolves, one cinnamon in color and the other blonde, joined Kaly. Teeth bared, the cinnamon wolf snapped at Asher, but Kaly bumped him with her hip, pushing him to the side. She seemed to be saying the fight with Asher was hers. Asher limped badly from the bite and burn he'd received from his first encounter with Kaly, leaving him at a distinct disadvantage. The scent of burnt fur permeated the air as the wolves faced off, exchanging bites.

Suleima dragged her gaze from the wolves to focus on the true threat: the Jorogumo. Using precious little of her power, she pulled at the earth, liquefying the ground beneath the Jorogumo, then dropped the power quickly, letting it solidify, trapping her legs.

Gage landed a bite on one of the Jorogumo's legs before dancing out of the way of her fangs. Two more wolves did the same from the other side. She let out an awful screech of pain, and the glow from her eyes faded.

Dynasira appeared a few moments later with the jinn, yelling to Suleima. The connection was severed. They called for Agron, the green-scaled dragon, who appeared in seconds, spraying the Jorogumo with acid. The Jorogumo was melting, letting out a screech of pain that made Suleima's skin crawl. Drops of acid flew through the air as the Jorogumo flailed in agony, forcing the wolves to try to dodge them.

The three traitor wolves howled and redoubled their aggression, charging Kaly's wolf as she backed away from the pool of acid. The black wolf was singed in several places. He had apparently wised up, and he was trying to keep his distance, while doing his best to corner Kaly and separate her from the rest of the pack.

Suleima yelled for Gage to get out of there, away from the acid. Gage growled, and instead of backing away, he headed to join Kaly's fight. He barreled into the three rogue wolves, knocking the whole group of them off balance, and bit the black wolf on the back knee, searing his flesh and crippling it. He jumped over the group, leaving the rest of the fight to Kaly and the other wolves, and moved to head off a new wave of orcs and goblins.

Suleima felt the pull.

Dirrin was using his spell. He realized he was losing his army and would need more power. He was going to sacrifice more of his creatures to gain more power. He was close, but not close enough. Behind her, she saw the Crystal Dragon, in human form. She motioned to him, as she pulled the ingredients from her pack, preparing her hands.

As he approached, she took a deep breath. One instant, he was human, the next, he was a dragon of immense size. He closed his claws around Suleima, completely swallowing her up. She was not prepared for it, but breathed deep and settled herself, waiting for whatever would come next. She was prepared to die, but hoped, by some miracle, she could survive this. She steeled herself against the nerves that threatened to overtake her. Their side had lost a few already. She felt the weight of that all the way to her soul. If she did not succeed, many more would be lost.

She could feel the shock reverberating through the sea of creatures below her, both from seeing the Crystal Dragon, and from watching nearly half of their numbers sacrificed to Dirrin for more power.

"It will be a long drop," was all the dragon said before opening his claw. Suleima pulled at the air, slowing her fall enough it would not be fatal, but fast enough to maintain her element of surprise. She felt the jolt of landing all the way up to her teeth. But she landed right behind Dirrin, and the Crystal Dragon circled him, drawing his attention away from Suleima.

Suleima started her spell. "It was not yours, not meant to be. You cannot steal. The power rejects. To its rightful place, it will return. Aided by crimson light and the Flame so true, the power no more belongs to you." By the time she finished speaking, she was yelling, facing Dirrin head-on. She felt him gathering his power to blast her with his fire, as she uncovered the crystal cupped between her hands. The crystal grew warm in her hands, then hot as it pulled in all of the magic Dirrin had stolen from others. She gritted her teeth. The crystal burned her hands. She saw and felt the spell as she closed her intention and the essence of those Dirrin had sacrificed left him. It brought tears to her eyes to see the vast number of them. How could one man do so much harm? A man taught by one of the greatest people she knew.

Where did it all go wrong?

Dirrin's eyes widened, then narrowed; hatred burned in their depths. He raised a hand, calling for the black dragons, who flew up and headed straight for her. Clan Azula headed her way with the Crystal Dragon to head them off. Dirrin sent fireballs hurtling at Suleima. She dodged what she could, taking the brunt of those she couldn't avoid on the left side, the scarring helping her to avoid some of the pain. She kept moving, trying to avoid the spells she could, trying to put him in a place of disadvantage. He was no longer practiced at conserving his power, he would run his own well dry soon enough.

She was running low on her power, even using the tricks Erist had taught her, but she called in a gust of wind, blowing him off balance, churning up dirt around him, disturbing his vision. Her full attention was on Dirrin, it had to be, but she heard the roars and hisses from the dragons fighting above, the screech of the thunderbirds, the growls of the wolves just past the tree line— a cacophony of noise that pounded at her, demanding her attention. But the burning hatred in Dirrin's eyes kept her focus despite the sounds surrounding her.

As soon as she released the power over air, Suleima pulled her bow, firing before Dirrin could regain his composure. The arrow hit his shoulder, and he roared in pain. He retaliated, throwing fireballs even faster at her. She took a quick deep breath, and then, using what she had learned on the mountain, created a vacuum of air surrounding her, snuffing out the fire before it reached her. She would not be able to hold it for long, so she waited for him to tire. She took the next hit, directly to her arm, then shoved the vacuum bubble at him, holding tightly to the spell.

She pulled another arrow, releasing the vacuum as she released the arrow, sinking it solidly into his thigh. As he cried out, Suleima hit him with another blast of air, knocking him off his feet.

Suleima nocked another arrow and ran to him, standing above him. "Surrender, Dirrin. This crusade of yours is a failure. You will be held responsible and punished for your actions. You must know this is over."

"How could you ever think I would surrender? And to you? I would rather die than surrender to you!"

"Why are you doing this? We were not taught this way."

"Erist was weak! You are weak!" he shouted.

Suleima turned around to see a black dragon heading straight for her. Dirrin blasted her with a fireball in the side, accidentally knocking her out of the path the dragon was on.

Dynasira opened her mouth, shooting boiling water at the black dragon, who screamed in pain. The Crystal Dragon blew out a gust of icy air, freezing the water around the black dragon, and then whipped his tail around and shattered the black dragon to pieces.

Suleima tried to get up, but the injury from the last fireball had likely broken several ribs and left a huge scorch mark. Dirrin struggled to his feet, pulling a fire ball as he did. As he prepared to release it directly at her head, Gage came out of nowhere. He leapt. Dirrin shifted, aiming directly at Gage. Suleima pulled back on her bow and fired an arrow, pushing desperately with air to direct the arrow and speed it up. It struck Dirrin in the side of the neck, dropping him to his knees. She hit an artery. Because of Dirrin's movement, Gage's aim was off the mark, and he landed a few feet away.

Suleima watched in horror. Dirrin fell face up on the ground, eyes wide and fixed. He was gone, and she had done it. She'd saved Gage, but she took the life of someone she knew and grew up with, someone she had thought of at one time as a good friend. The creatures he had summoned and sent after her were evil creatures who would not stop until she was dead, but they were never her friend. Despite the pain in her side, Suleima brought her knees up, hugging them to her and hiding her face. She couldn't bear seeing his death stare. The sounds of battle seemed to quiet and become more distant. Whether from her shock or the battle losing steam, she couldn't be sure.

She felt Gage approach. He sat next to her, his side touching her uninjured one. His head swung back and forth, keeping watch over her, ready to protect her if anything approached. She steadied herself with a deep breath, packed away her feelings to be dealt with later, and did her best to stand.

Gage growled when she winced and whimpered, unable to stop herself as the pain lanced through her side at the movement. But she got to her feet and steadied herself, gripping her bow, a new arrow nocked. Her magic was dangerously low.

She looked around and didn't see much movement. She could hear some commotion in the woods behind her, but it *was* a lot quieter since Dirrin's death. She was moving slower than she would have liked, but she moved toward the most noise. She had only taken a few steps when the Crystal Dragon landed in front of her. In the next moment, he stood before her in human form.

"You have done what you set out to do, Suleima," he said. "Dirrin is dead. He can no longer hurt others for his own gain. The remaining creatures and people who followed him have almost all been captured or killed. The remaining shamans and jinn are rounding up the last of the necromancers. The Shwara dragons have been destroyed. There is nothing left for me to do here; the balance has been restored. I must return to my mountain, with my Flame."

"Thank you for all of the help you have provided us. For helping me to see Erist again and learn from him. Without your help, this fight would have ended much differently." Suleima handed the red crystal back to the dragon.

"If you ever have need of the Flame again, it will be right where you found it. You only need to prove yourself true," he replied. In an instant, he was airborne and gone.

Suleima sighed, her body and mind exhausted from the events of the day. She slowly made her way to the area where the ent, Jorogumo and cyclops fell. The jinn and shamans who were not tending to wounds were gathering up the remains of the fallen creatures.

Dynasira landed and approached her. "Once all of the remains are collected and brought here, we will be sure to destroy them, so no necromancer can bring them back. The thunderbird who was bit first by the Jorogumo was lost. The healers were not able to save him. The other thunderbirds left to take his body back to their home. We lost one of the Amarola dragons to the Schwara dragons. One of the Rojada dragons was seriously injured by the cyclops, before it got to you. She is being treated by the shamans and jinn." She paused a moment before turning to Gage. "The three wolves who went missing from your pack joined up with Dirrin. They were killed, as well as the other wolf who fought with them. Kaly is in rough shape. She took a hit from the Jorogumo venom. Somehow, she managed to fight through the pain and weakness, taking out those wolves. One of the thunderbirds managed to get her to a healer as soon as the last of those wolves fell. She will have a tough recovery, but it looks like she has done that before. A couple other wolves also had minor injuries and the wolf hit by the cyclops's club was lost. Somehow, we made it out of here without too many casualties. We all worked very well together."

"Thanks, Dyna," Suleima said, wincing at the effort it took to speak.

"Let's get you to one of the shamans," she said, reaching for Suleima.

Gage growled.

"I'll be OK," Suleima said, stepping between the two. "I can get to them on my own if I need them. I prefer to heal without magic. I have used quite enough of it today, I think."

The cleanup took longer than she hoped, but she had to be there as the de facto leader of this group. She visited with the wolves and the Rojada dragon in the tent the shamans had set up. She allowed the shamans to help her clean and bandage her new wounds but refused to allow them to use their magic to heal her. Those more gravely wounded would need their attention. She spent time at Kaly's bedside.

When the group gathered to observe the pyre of the fallen, Suleima stood quietly. Dirrin topped the pile. Gage stood next to her. A separate pyre would be built the following day for the allies they had lost. They would not be dishonored by being burned with those who caused the battle.

Suleima sat to conserve some of her energy and stared into the pyre. So many lost senselessly. So many who believed they were better than the rest, believing they should rule over others. How had it come to this? How was there such evil in the world? She knew that Erist sheltered her from a lot of the evil in the world, but it had seemed to escalate so quickly. Was there always this unrest and she just didn't see it?

That had to change. Now. She had not fought this battle, sacrificed so much, to allow this kind of toxicity to exist without trying to change it.

Chapter 25

As the last of the embers died, Suleima slowly stood and stepped forward, calling for the attention of everyone present. "We have several people we have captured or who have surrendered to us through this ordeal. We need to decide what is to be done with them."

"Kill them all!" came a shout from the back.

"We cannot kill them just because they chose the wrong side. If we do, we are no better than Dirrin," she replied. "We need to find a group of people who will be unbiased and fair. Any punishment handed out needs to fit the crime."

Dynasira stepped forward, "I think you should lead the group, Suleima."

"We need to decide as a group who we think should hold positions in this group, or council, or whatever we call it. Then, the ones within the group should decide who they wish to lead. We should have representatives from each of our groups. I believe at least one or two of each would be best."

"Clan Rojada has a holding area available for those in custody now. It is magic free, so it will be safe for keeping those with magic from escaping," the leader of the Rojada dragons spoke up.

"There is one other, a necromancer caught before the battle. She is currently in a holding room at the pack house for the Amber Mountain Pack. I would be grateful if you could take her." Suleima addressed him.

"Certainly. I speak for Clan Rojada. We would nominate Dynasira of Clan Azula to represent us on the council. She has done much to assist and organize this battle. We feel she would represent us fairly," he added.

Nods from several other dragons in attendance confirmed it.

Hamanad stepped forward. "I would represent the jinn on this council."

Gage stepped forward. He announced that as Alpha, he, and Kaly, when she was recovered, would join the council.

One of the shaman healers stepped forward, "Suleima is our choice to represent us."

"We have a start. Let's all go home and get healed. We can meet up in a day or two, to discuss options for the people in custody and finalize who we want to have representing each group. Anyone is welcome at the meeting." Suleima felt the strain of the day and her injuries pulling at her. She made a move to step back and nearly fell as her knees gave out. Gage was right there to steady her.

"I offer up the pack house to be used for the meeting. For now, we need to return. Clan Rojada, you are welcome tonight to pick up the necromancer in our cell. One of my wolves will show you where she is and assist you in getting her out." Gage held her arm and escorted Suleima away from the group. The moment they were out of sight of the group, he lifted her into his arms.

"You can't carry me the entire way," she protested.

"You would be surprised at what I could do if I needed to," Gage responded.

"Let me help with that," Dynasira said, coming out of the dark on their right. Dynasira shifted. "I will carry her home, Gage. I will get you settled, head off to meet with the clans, and you can rest."

Dynasira slowly descended and dropped Suleima gently on the ground before shifting and helping her up. Suleima reached out, making sure her wards were in place, as she had no power left to strengthen them. She took Dynasira's arm to steady herself as she entered the cabin.

"I can wait here a while. I don't need to meet with the clan leaders tonight. It could wait until tomorrow."

"Gage is on his way. He has somehow managed to get back to the pack house and into a car already. I can sense him not far away," she replied. "I don't need both of you here. If you can, help me get ingredients for my recharging spell. I left my pack out at the pyre. It didn't cross my mind to pick it up."

"I'll fly back out and get it," Dynasira said. She gathered the items Suleima would need and placed them on the small table near the water pump.

"You're a great friend. I don't know what I would do without you. I don't know what I would have done without you today, Dyna," she said. "I do have one favor to ask."

"Anything."

"Can you return tomorrow? When I recharge, I'll be out of it for a long while. I am fully drained; besides the fact I was injured. I don't want Gage stuck out here while I am unconscious, and he will not leave while I am."

"You have that right," he said from the still open doorway.

Dynasira headed out the door. "Take care of her. I'll bring your pack of supplies with me tomorrow."

Gage approached Suleima as she stood at the sink, wondering if she would have the strength to pump the water from the well.

"Are you OK?" he asked.

"I will be. I just need to recharge and rest."

"I'll be right here. You do what you need to and then rest. Tomorrow will take care of itself," he said, resting his hand on her shoulder. He stepped back then, allowing her to perform her spell, standing nearby if she needed him, but far enough so he wasn't in the way.

As the final sparks fell, she lay on her bed finally at peace, a small smile on her face. *He was right,* she thought to herself. *The council, the next steps, rebuilding peace in their community, Gage—it will all sort itself out, tomorrow.*

Epilogue

Suleima walked gingerly into the clearing. Her injuries from the previous day's battle were taking their toll, but she needed to keep moving. Gage and Dynasira were right behind her. There were a few hastily erected tents, trash littering the ground, and general chaos.

"Agron found this as we were out rounding up any stragglers from the battle. This was the main camp for Dirrin and his group," Dynasira said, kicking at some of the trash. "We've kept watch since we found it. No one in or out. That one, over there, was Dirrin's."

Suleima headed in that direction. Most of the army green tents were leaning one way or the other, but Dirrin's, largest of all, stood as if it had been meticulously built. She reached out with her senses to find any hint of a ward but found nothing. There was nothing around camp either.

She entered his tent alone to be sure that she hadn't missed a spell, but when there were no consequences, Suleima motioned for Gage and Dynasira to follow her inside. They were there to gather any of Dirrin's spell books or writings that could be used to give rise to Dirrin's movement again with a new leader.

The inside of the tent was fairly spacious. There was a large trunk at the foot of Dirrin's large cot and a cabinet similar to the one Suleima kept in her own cabin. Transporting those would not have been easy. The trunk lid was open, as were the doors of the cabinet and its drawers. Each stood empty.

"No one has approached the camp since we found it," Dynasira stated flatly. "They must have been here before the battle ended."

Suleima nodded, walked to the chest, and reached a hand out, opening her senses. "There are old spells on the chest and cabinet. I sense their remnants. They were disabled without being triggered. Someone powerful enough to neutralize his wards took all of Dirrin's books."

Thank you for joining me and my imaginary friends on their journey! I truly hope you enjoyed it! This has been a labor of love. Love these characters? Come find me on my website for updates on new books.

You can also sign up for my newsletter there and receive a free prequel scene Elements: A Moment in Time. The story of Erist's death.

About the author

I have been writing since I was in high school and have finally found the courage to put some of that writing out for all to see. I have a love of all things artistic and crafty. Reading books, watching movies and listening to music makes my heart happy. I am a self proclaimed Jack of All Trades, Master of None. I live in the mid-west with my husband, two amazing and crazy kids, and a cat who we think is part squirrel.

Acknowledgements

First, thank you to all of you who have read this book through to the end. Thank you for coming along on this journey with me! I truly hope you enjoyed it. Hopefully there will be many more adventures together in our futures!

This book would have never been possible without the support of my amazing husband and beautiful daughters. They put up with this crazy idea from concept to launch (which was a much longer process than they ever bargained for)! I can never thank them enough. To my husband, my first alpha reader, thank you for helping to bounce story ideas off of and helping me identify my 'that' problem.

To my Yas, I cannot express how much your support and cheer-leading helped to get me through the imposter syndrome moments.

And a special thank you to the QueenYa for all of your help in 'fixing' my attempts to create a cover, logo, bookmark, etc. and advice on creating my small business!

To my Author Ever After community, thank you for lighting the fire under me and helping to walk me through the intimidating process of self-publishing. Without you, this novel would still be sitting in a file on my computer (as it has since 2021).